Vanishing Point

by Ben M. Baglio

Interior art by Doris Ettlinger

SCHOLASTIC INC.

New York   Toronto   London   Auckland   Sydney
Mexico City   New Delhi   Hong Kong   Buenos Aires

Special thanks to Lucy Courtenay

ISBN-13: 978-0-439-87145-7
ISBN-10: 0-439-87145-X

12 11 10 9 8 7 6 5 4 3 2 1   7 8 9 10 11 12/0

Printed in the U.S.A.   40
First Scholastic printing, April 2007

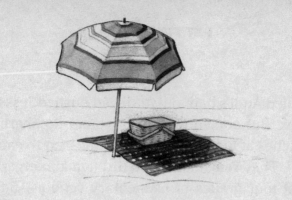

Chapter One

Andi Talbot craned her neck to get a better view from the backseat of the rental car her mom was driving. They were on vacation, visiting their old hometown of Coral Point, Florida, and Andi knew that any minute now she'd see the Atlantic Ocean. The sea in Florida was very different from that of Washington State, where Andi and her mom lived now. Here it was frothy and green and warm, unlike the wild gray waves of the Pacific Northwest. But even better than seeing the familiar warm waves would be seeing her old friend Jess Martin. Andi couldn't wait!

"We should be at Jess's house in twenty minutes," Andi's mom, Judy Talbot, called from the front seat.

Andi and Jess Martin had been best friends since kindergarten. Things hadn't started too well, Andi remembered with a grin. On the first morning of school Jess

1

had pulled Andi's hair and Andi had pushed Jess into the sandbox. But somehow they'd wound up sharing their sandwiches at lunch break and sitting next to each other in class. They remained close through kindergarten and the first four grades of elementary school—until Andi and her mom moved to Orchard Park in Seattle. Andi and Jess had kept in touch by e-mail, but that wasn't the same as talking at least five times a day the way they used to. Andi felt a sudden twinge of nervousness. What if Jess didn't want to be her friend anymore?

Sensing Andi's mood, the little tan-and-white terrier on her lap sat up and started licking her face.

"Buddy!" Andi laughed. "Okay, so you were an angel on the plane. That doesn't mean you can lick me to death now!" Feeling better, she settled down and pressed her nose against the car window, watching for landmarks and stroking Buddy's rough tan head.

Andi had offered to board Buddy at the kennels in Orchard Park, but Jess had insisted that he come, too. "He's so cute," she told Andi. "I'm looking forward to seeing Bud almost as much as I'm looking forward to seeing you." Mrs. Talbot had called Jess's mom to make sure it was okay for him to come. Andi scratched the top of his head, glad that he hadn't been left behind. Buddy would enjoy visiting all their old places—especially the beach.

"There's the scuba shop!" she exclaimed. "Hey! What's that next to it?" A large white building with a wavelike steel sculpture on its roof stood where a furniture store had been before.

"I guess Coral Point has changed since we lived here," her mom replied. "Nothing stays the same, not even people."

Andi didn't know about that. Besides starting the Pet Finders Club in Orchard Park with her new friends Natalie Lewis and Tristan Saunders, she was exactly the same. Wasn't she?

The roads were narrowing now, and they passed between tall buildings painted in various pastel shades. The tarmac shimmered in the heat, and palm trees waved overhead. Then she spotted a glimmer of silver on the horizon.

"The ocean!" Andi and Jess and Buddy had spent so much time by the sea with their friends—it had been their whole life.

Buddy barked and Andi realized that they were driving down a very familiar road. Buddy sat upright next to her, one paw on the seat in front of him, his ears pricked and alert. It seemed as if the road was familiar to him, too.

"It all looks exactly the same!" Andi gasped, staring

at the street where she and her mom had once lived. "Look—the Mendozas still haven't painted their porch! And there's the Thompsons' house and . . ." She reeled off the names of all their old neighbors. She and Jess had lived right at the end of the street—Andi and her mom in a pink single-story house and Jess and her family in the yellow one next door.

A lump rose in Andi's throat when she saw a bright green pickup parked in the pink house's driveway, where her mom's car had always stood.

The front door of the yellow house swung open with a bang. A girl with short, curly dark hair and sparkling brown eyes ran out onto the porch. Peeping around from behind her were two little boys, nearly identical with their straight black bangs and devilish smiles.

"Jess!" Andi scrambled out of the backseat and ran to greet her old friend. Halfway up the porch steps, she stopped, overcome with a strange feeling of shyness.

"Hey," said Jess, looking as if she felt awkward, too.

"Hey yourself," Andi said. She wondered when Jess had gotten her ears pierced. Her friend looked taller and her hair was shorter than it used to be. There was a weird pause and Andi was thankful when a slender, pretty woman with Jess's same curly hair came onto the porch to join them.

"The Talbots return!" Annalisa Martin embraced Andi and her mom. "You must be exhausted after your trip. There's some cold lemonade on the back porch, and Jess and I have been making pecan cookies. They were always your favorite, Andi."

Inside the Martins' house, Andi gazed around at the familiar furniture and the frayed hall rug. Everything looked the same.

"Watch the rug," Jess joked from behind her.

Andi laughed. The rug had always been a standing joke between them, as Andi had fallen over it a hundred times in the past. Maybe things were going to be the same after all.

Jess's younger brothers, Jamie and Jonjo, scampered past, shooting shy glances at Andi as they followed their mom and Mrs. Talbot into the kitchen.

Jess produced a doggy treat for Buddy. "Hey, Bud," she said, hunkering down to stroke Buddy's back.

Andi noticed that she'd remembered Buddy's favorite scratching spot: just between the shoulder blades. Buddy wriggled with delight and pushed against Jess's hands.

"This is weird, huh?" Jess said, echoing Andi's thoughts.

"Uh-huh." Andi felt a little easier when she realized

that Jess was feeling strange as well. They stared at each other and grinned.

Jess rose to her feet and linked arms with Andi. "Come on," she said. "Let's join everyone out back before Jamie and Jonjo eat all the cookies."

The Martins' yard looked the same as ever, full of vibrant hibiscus bushes and their trumpetlike flowers. The turquoise swimming pool gleamed in one corner; the swing and slide were in the same place, and the old sandbox was, too. A baseball and mitt lay abandoned on the grass, as if Andi had just pitched for Jamie and Jonjo the way she always used to.

"Andi!" Jamie shouted, running into the yard and fetching the glove and ball. "Wanna play?"

Andi grinned. "Maybe later, Jamie, okay?" she said.

"You always used to say that!" Jamie complained.

"And I always pitched for you in the end, didn't I?" Andi countered.

"I guess," Jamie said. Then he ran over to the slide with Jonjo.

Over lemonade and cookies, Andi found herself relaxing with Jess. Her old friend was chattering at full speed, telling Andi about their former classmates.

"You remember Beth? She had to get glasses last week. And that little guy David, who always sat at the back of the room? He's the tallest boy in our class now. And hey, you remember Chloe and Suki, right?"

Andi snorted. "Sure, I remember them," she said. "They were total snobs, weren't they? They always had weird expressions on their faces—like they were smelling something really, really gross, right?" She looked at Jess and grinned, expecting her friend to grin back.

"I don't know about that." Jess took a long drink of lemonade. "But since you left, I made friends with them. They're into the coolest things. Chloe got the cutest bathing suit for the summer," she gushed. "She says her dad bought it in the Bahamas. I'd totally *die* to get one just like it."

"It's just a swimsuit," Andi joked, putting down her lemonade. "Death is a bit drastic, don't you think?"

Jess stared at her oddly, and Andi got the feeling she'd just said something wrong.

Mrs. Talbot glanced at her watch. "Well, thanks for everything, Annalisa," she said, standing up. "I'd better go. Margot's expecting me." Mrs. Talbot was staying with an old colleague two blocks away, and now Andi wasn't so sure she wanted her mom to leave her there.

"I'll call you in the morning," she promised, kissing Andi as they all followed her out to the car. "Are you and Jess planning on heading down to the beach?"

"You bet," said Jess promptly.

"Sure." Andi bent down and ruffled Buddy's ears. "Bud needs a walk."

"Walk?" Jess echoed. "I hope you mean run, Andi. My running shoes are ready and waiting!"

With a sudden flash of gladness, Andi remembered the way she and Jess had always run up and down the boardwalk on the beach with Buddy. They'd been on the track team together at school and used to have races on the sand. "I'll still be faster than you," she warned.

Jess's eyes gleamed at the challenge. "Don't be so sure," she said, poking Andi in the ribs.

They waved good-bye to Andi's mom after they unloaded Andi's luggage from the car. Then Jess helped Andi carry her bags inside.

"We're sharing," Jess told Andi as they walked down the hallway to Jess's bedroom at the side of the house. Buddy stayed close to Andi's heels, sniffing along the corridor. "It'll be just like when we had sleepovers!" Jess stopped and squeezed Andi's arm. "I'm really glad to see you again, Andi," she said. "I know everything's a little different, but before the week is over, you'll feel like you never left!"

Andi grinned and put her arm around Jess's neck, deciding to forget all about Jess's weird reaction earlier. "Sounds great," she said.

"Oh, and guess what." Jess looked at her expectantly.

Andi rolled her eyes. Jess always loved making her guess stuff. "You booked us a trip to the moon from Kennedy Space Center?"

"Better," said Jess, looking triumphant. "I've organized a pool party for you on Tuesday! All your old friends are coming, Andi. They were so psyched when I told them you were staying with me. It'll be just like old times!"

"Cool!" Andi cried, happy that her old friend had gone to all the trouble. Then she and Jess rushed to put on their running shoes and take Buddy down to the beach. Before Andi knew it, she and Jess were pounding along the familiar route, breathing the fresh sea air.

Andi awoke early Sunday morning to warm sunlight playing across Jess's ceiling. Getting out of bed, she wandered to the window, which looked directly across to her old house—and her old bedroom window.

Across the fence, the drapes in the pink house were still drawn. Andi's old drapes had been a beautiful soft lilac, but these drapes were quite different: dark blue, with a yellow-flecked pattern. Andi felt a little relieved. Although the house looked familiar, she thought of Orchard Park as home now. She stared, thinking about the person who was sleeping right where her old bed used to be.

"That's Zack's room." Jess stood next to her, yawning in the morning light. "His family moved in a couple weeks after you left. He's really nice."

Andi felt an odd wave of jealousy as she thought of Zack and Jess making friends.

"It's not the same as having you there, though," Jess added. "He doesn't know flashlight Morse code!"

Andi grinned. She and Jess used to signal to each other across the way with their flashlights—on, off, on again, like fireflies in the night. "What's he like?" she asked.

"He's a year older than we are," Jess said as they pulled on their clothes and went downstairs to find some breakfast. "And he's totally into tennis. He also has a cute Chihuahua named Huck. Hey, why don't we go over and say hello after breakfast? I'm sure you want to look around your old house, right? I know I would."

Downstairs, Andi found some dog food waiting on the counter, beside a brand-new dog bowl. "This is Buddy's favorite food!" she said, glancing at Jess. "You remembered!"

Jess beamed. "Like I'd forget!"

Buddy wolfed down his breakfast—and Andi did the

same with hers. The sea air made her extra hungry, and eating waffles on Jess's sunny back porch made her feel as though her vacation had truly begun.

Mrs. Martin stepped onto the deck, holding out the receiver. "Andi, your mom's on the phone."

Andi took it. "Hey, Mom," she said. "Isn't it great, having breakfast in the sun?"

"I'm glad you're settling in okay," Judy Talbot said. "I was a little worried about you when I left yesterday. I know it must be strange, seeing Jess again after all this time."

Andi glanced across the table at Jess, who was fussing over Buddy. "It is strange," she admitted, "but nice at the same time."

"So what are you doing today?" Mrs. Talbot asked.

Andi told her mom that Jess was taking her over to see their old house.

"How nice!" Mrs. Talbot sounded wistful. "I want to hear all the details, okay?"

"Sure," Andi said. "Are you getting along with Margot?"

"Same as you." Andi could hear the smile in her mom's voice. "Strange, but nice at the same time."

Chapter Two

"Are you nervous about visiting your old house?" Jess asked as she, Andi, and Buddy walked down the Martins' driveway after breakfast.

"I thought I would be," Andi admitted. She glanced at the white daisies that grew in a familiar sprawl along the front porch of the pink house. "But seeing Zack's drapes this morning helped me remember that this isn't my house anymore." Still, even Andi had to admit that it was weird to be ringing the doorbell at her old front door.

"Hi, guys." A tall, thin boy opened the door. He had very short blond hair and a crooked smile. "This must be Andi, right? Come on in."

Andi stepped into her old hallway and stared around. The colors were completely different from when she had lived there. Her mom had painted everything in pale sandy yellows and blues—but Zack's parents had bright reds and oranges everywhere. There was a neat hall table where the Talbots' old bookcase had once stood. Instead of rugs on the floor, the whole house looked like it had been newly carpeted. And it smelled different, too. She looked at the pictures on the walls and the collection of unfamiliar coats and jackets on a coatrack, and part of her wondered if she'd ever lived there at all.

Then she caught sight of a scuff mark along a floorboard. "Hey, I did that!" she exclaimed. "I was running down the hall too fast and caught my foot. I was wearing my red sneakers, and my sole marked the white paint!"

"Oh, so that was you!" Zack started to laugh. "Mom thought it was my fault. We didn't notice it at first."

A tiny dog with enormous ears trotted out of the kitchen, its black eyes like bright buttons on its cute face. The Chihuahua stopped at the sight of Buddy, who lay down and rolled on the carpet in a friendly way. The tiny dog came over and sniffed at him with interest.

"This is Buddy," Andi said. Laughing, she added, "It's pretty rare for him to be the big dog in a doggy encounter." She reached out to pet the little Chihuahua. "And you must be Huck. Aren't you cute?"

By the time they finished fussing over Buddy and

Huck, Andi had decided that she liked Zack. He had a nice smile and a relaxed, laid-back attitude. She found she could talk to him quite easily about Coral Point and his school and, of course, the main thing they had in common: the house.

"Jess tells me you used to have my room," Zack said, leading the way down the hall. "I have to warn you: it looks pretty different now."

He opened the door. Andi stared at the dark blue room. Her room had been lilac, just like her drapes, with a border of dolphins around the top of the walls. Now there were tennis posters stuck up around the room, and Andi realized that the yellow pattern on the dark blue drapes was made up of tiny yellow tennis balls. Two rackets were propped up beside the bed, which stood against a different wall from where she'd had hers.

"It sure is different," Andi agreed, taking in the bookcase bending under sports annuals and the PlayStation in the corner. "I guess lilac wasn't your color."

Zack laughed. "Not really."

"Let's take the dogs to the beach," Jess suggested. "Are you busy today, Zack?"

Zack ran his hand through his hair. "I have a tennis lesson this afternoon, but I don't have anything right now," he said.

"Why don't you come with us?" Andi glanced down at Buddy and Huck, who were chasing each other around the bedroom, lying flat on the carpet one minute and racing full tilt the next. "Bring Huck, too. It'll be nice for Buddy to have a friend on his vacation."

Zack went to tell his mom that they were heading for the beach while Andi and Jess ran back to Jess's house to gather their beach things.

Within ten minutes, they were on the boardwalk by the sea. Andi kicked off her flip-flops and ran to the edge of the water.

"Brr!" she laughed. "It's colder than I remember!"

"It's still early," Jess reminded her. "This is dog-walking time, not sunbathing time. Check it out!" She flung out her arm at the near-empty beach and then at the boardwalk. There were plenty of people out that morning, jogging, blading, and strolling along. At least half of them were walking dogs. Andi was amused to see how different the dogs in Florida were from the dogs in Orchard Park. Back home, everyone seemed to have big shaggy hunting dogs whose thick coats were perfectly designed for the cool weather. Here, most of the dogs seemed to be in miniature, with ribbons around their necks and short, gleaming fur. There were large dogs, too, but they were definitely in the minority.

One large dog in particular caught Andi's attention: a glossy, young-looking German shepherd with a fine-boned head and wonderful long, pricked ears. His coat gleamed in the sunshine as if it had been oiled, and he raced along the boardwalk with his owner like a Thoroughbred, leaping enthusiastically after low-flying seagulls.

Buddy barked, and Andi looked down at him. He was lying with his nose between his paws, his back legs straight and ready to run.

"You want me to throw a ball, huh?" Andi said, remembering how often she used to play catch with Buddy on this beach. She ruffled his fur, and Buddy barked with excitement, snuffling his nose farther down between his paws.

"Here!" Jess called, producing a red rubber ball from her backpack. "Catch, Bud!"

Buddy tore after the ball, with Huck running gamely behind.

"This is probably the most exercise Huck's ever had," Zack joked a while later, as they sat on the boardwalk and dangled their legs over the edge, watching the two dogs chase each other across the sand.

"Here, let's take a picture!" Jess fished in her bag and brought out her digital camera. She snapped a couple of shots of the dogs and then jumped down onto the sand to snap a couple more of Andi and Zack.

"I'll take some shots of you guys now," Zack offered, holding out his hand for the camera.

"Let's pose!" Jess yelled, then struck a dramatic stance with her head thrown back and her hips jutting out to one side.

Zack snapped away, saying things like "Great!" and "Terrific!" while Andi and Jess practiced posing and running in slow motion and as many other silly things as they could think of.

"Stop!" Andi begged, breathless with laughter. "I'm going to burst."

Jess dragged her by the arm. "Come on," she said. "Let's take a few more down by the marina."

"We could pretend we're going cruising on a fancy yacht," Andi suggested, really getting into the game as they ran along the boardwalk with Buddy and Huck at their heels.

Jess tossed her head in a supermodel kind of way. "Who's pretending?" She grinned.

The marina was a bit farther down the beach, where the sand stopped and a row of pontoons curved away from the shore. Boats were lined up at anchor, their halyards clinking gently in the breeze. There were dinghies and sloops, jaunty little speedboats and really enormous yachts that dwarfed the low buildings that clustered around the harbor. Palm trees waved their dark green fronds, and the water sloshed and murmured beneath the silvery wooden walkways.

Jess stopped beside one of the yachts—a sleek white boat with a blue stripe running around its hull and the name *Lemming* painted in dramatic lettering down the side. She adjusted her sunglasses, placed one hand on the boat's railing, and put the other hand on her hip. "Bahamas, here I come!" she shouted as Andi ran over to join her.

Zack lifted the camera and snapped a couple of shots while Andi tried to stop laughing and look more like a glamour queen than a breathless kid.

"Say, Carl," came a woman's voice from high up on the deck. "I didn't know we were taking anyone else along on our trip!"

Andi turned scarlet with embarrassment as she realized the beautiful red-haired woman standing on the deck of the *Lemming* must have heard everything they'd said.

An Asian man in his late twenties, with dark hair and a deep mahogany tan, leaned on the rail beside the woman and smiled down at Andi and the others. "Hey there," he said. "You guys like the *Lemming*, huh?"

"This is so humiliating," Jess whispered, tugging at Andi's sleeve. "If Chloe and Suki ever heard about this . . . Come on, Andi, let's get out of here!"

"Sorry!" Andi managed a half smile at the couple standing on the deck of the *Lemming* before Jess towed her away. They caught up with Zack a hundred yards farther down the dock, where he was buying ice-cream cones.

"Thanks for sticking around," Jess huffed.

"I figured you could handle that on your own." Zack grinned. "But here's something to make up for it." He handed Jess and Andi each a cone. "Let's snag that table over there."

"I guess we'll forgive you . . . this time," Andi said as they flopped down at the wooden table beside the water. She licked her cone as Buddy begged politely at her feet, his back as straight as an arrow. Andi laughed when Huck tried the same trick but toppled over in an undignified kind of way.

"This is *soooo* relaxing." Jess sighed, leaning back with her eyes closed so that she could feel the sun on her cheeks. "I come here most days, but it feels different with you guys. More like a real vacation."

Andi munched down to the tip of her cone. She was about to split the remains between Buddy and Huck when she saw a third dog sitting a little farther from their table, watching her hungrily. It was the glossy young German shepherd she'd seen running down the boardwalk.

Up close, he was even more handsome. His coat was short and sleek and he rippled with muscles as he shifted his weight from one foot to the other. Andi admired the way the tan patches on his back graduated to a gorgeous coppery color on his chest and belly and beneath his tail, while the black on his back and head shone almost dark blue in the sun. He was posing so beautifully that Andi pointed her camera at him and clicked the shutter.

"Oh, please forgive my daughter's dog!" a voice said from the other side of their table. "He has no manners!"

Andi turned to see a well-built man with thick dark hair and a strong, muscular body. He looked around fifty and was dressed in a royal blue CORAL POINT MARINA T-shirt and white running shorts. He pushed his sunglasses to the top of his head and smiled at them.

"No problem," Andi said as Buddy and Huck shared the last inch of her cone. "He's beautiful. Did you say he belonged to your daughter?"

"I'm dog-sitting," the man explained. "Susan's on vacation in Seattle this week, and I offered to look after

Laser." He bent down and ran his hand along Laser's sleek head.

"Seattle!" Andi exclaimed. "That's where I live!"

The man laughed at the coincidence. "I'm a Sunshine State guy through and through," he confided. "But I hear Seattle has its good points."

The man's name was Jim Harding, and he kept a sailing sloop called the *Happy Jack* on the far side of the marina. "I sail the *Happy Jack* most weekends if I can," he said. "Did I see you taking pictures by the *Lemming* a little earlier? She's quite a beauty, isn't she?"

"I guess." Andi felt herself blushing again as she remembered the couple on the *Lemming*'s deck. She busied herself petting Laser, who had wriggled closer to the table and was now looking at Andi with adoring deep brown eyes. Buddy growled jealously while Huck retreated beneath Zack's seat.

"So how are you planning to spend your vacation?" Jim Harding asked as he snapped a leash onto Laser's collar. "You should take in the Kennedy Space Center if you can—or maybe try some dolphin watching. Seeing how you like boats, I could always take you out to sea in the *Happy Jack*—if your mom is okay with it, of course. And the new SeaLife Center's supposed to be terrific."

"It is!" Zack nodded enthusiastically. "My cousin Shannon works there. It just opened a couple weeks ago," he added, turning to Andi.

"Thanks," Andi said to the older man, "but I'm not really a tourist. I used to live in Coral Point. I'm just visiting old friends."

Jim Harding raised his eyebrows. "In that case, welcome back! And if you do feel like a trip along the coast, get your mom to give me a call," he said, pulling out a business card, which he passed to Andi. "Any friend of Laser's is a friend of mine!"

Andi gave Laser one last pet as Jim whistled for the German shepherd to heel. Laser's coat felt gorgeous beneath her fingers, all smooth and warm and shiny. The German shepherd stood reluctantly and, after one last glance at the ice-cream stand, bounded after Jim with a steady, loping stride.

"What a beautiful dog," Andi murmured, watching Laser and Jim Harding until they were out of view. Buddy whined from somewhere near her feet. Looking down with a smile, Andi opened her arms, and the little terrier bounded onto her lap. "Don't worry, Bud," she said, dropping a kiss on the terrier's head. "Florida dogs may be pretty, but I'm not about to replace you!"

Chapter Three

"How about doing something tomorrow morning?" Zack suggested when they reached the front door of the pink house a little while later. "We could go to the SeaLife Center. I told you my cousin Shannon works there, right? She can get us in for free!"

"Or we could ask our parents if we can go sailing with Mr. Harding," Andi suggested hopefully.

Zack's face fell. "I'd love that, but I have a tennis lesson tomorrow afternoon," he said. "I think we'd need a whole day for a sailing trip. I mean, you could go without me, but . . ." He trailed off, looking disappointed.

"No way," Andi said. "We'll go sailing with Mr. Harding and Laser another day. The SeaLife Center sounds cool."

Jess didn't seem so sure. "I was hoping to go to the mall tomorrow," she admitted. "Remember, Andi? I told you I wanted to get a bathing suit like Chloe's." She turned to Zack. "We're having a pool party on Tuesday afternoon, Zack. Want to come?"

"Definitely!" Zack agreed. "Well, see you tomorrow at nine," he said, entering the house. "Mom'll give us a ride to the aquarium."

"We'll be there," Andi promised. She was relieved that they wouldn't be going shopping, but as Zack closed the door, she noticed that Jess was pouting.

"So much for the mall," Jess grumbled as they made their way to Jess's front porch. "Don't you want to look good on Tuesday, Andi? I mean, Suki and Chloe are going to be there."

Andi suppressed a sigh. "Come on, Jess. Who cares what we're wearing in a pool?"

Jess pouted a little more. "*I* do," she said, tucking her dark curls behind her ears.

"You sound just like my friend Natalie back at home," Andi joked, pushing open Jess's front door. "She always looks gorgeous. Just like you."

Just as Andi had hoped, Jess smiled at the compliment. "Well, I guess we still have time to go shopping, and I haven't been to the SeaLife Center yet, either," she said at last. "It could be cool. Zack's really nice, isn't he?" she added. "Suki and Chloe will be so impressed when they find out we're friends with an older kid."

"Really?" Andi asked, not knowing what the big deal was.

Jess nodded, then gasped. "Wouldn't it be awesome if Chloe and Suki haven't been to the SeaLife Center yet? I could be the first person to tell them all about it!" Looking more cheerful, she led the way into the house.

Andi followed, becoming thoughtful. She didn't like the way Jess was always trying to impress Chloe and Suki. She couldn't imagine worrying about friends that way. But at least now Jess was excited about going to the SeaLife Center!

Coral Point's new SeaLife Center turned out to be the white building with the wave-shaped sculpture that Andi had noticed on the way into town. There were huge dark blue plate glass windows all the way along its facade, and a mosaic of a leaping dolphin stretched above the glass doors. Although it was only nine-thirty, the parking lot was already half full.

Andi had left Buddy with Jess's mom, and Zack's mom dropped off the kids at the SeaLife Center. She'd be back to get them in time for lunch, when they'd have a picnic on the beach.

"Hey!" Zack exclaimed as his mom drove off. He stared

at a young German shepherd who sat tethered in the shade beside the big glass doors to the aquarium. "Is that Laser?"

The big dog was friendly enough, but up close Andi could see that it wasn't Laser at all. "The tan patches on this dog's coat are paler than Laser's coppery fur," she said, feeling a little disappointed. "And look—it's got four black paws. Laser had three black ones and a copper one."

"How do you remember details like what color paws Laser had?" Jess asked.

"From being in the Pet Finders Club," Andi explained. "You know, the club I set up with Natalie and Tristan in Orchard Park?"

Jess nodded, but Andi could tell that she wasn't very interested. For a moment, Andi felt annoyed with her old friend. The Pet Finders Club was one of the most important parts of Andi's life in Orchard Park, and she often e-mailed Jess about it.

"Pet Finders Club?" Zack echoed. "That sounds cool. Do you find people's dogs and cats for them?"

"And other pets," Andi said, pleased at Zack's interest. "Rabbits, horses—we even found a boa constrictor once! And . . ."

She broke off as a heavy truck thundered past, then

slowed to a crawl and turned in along the side of the SeaLife Center. A line of trucks were parked there with their back doors open. "Check out all those deliveries!" Zack exclaimed. "Shannon said the aquarium was still expanding and she wasn't joking!"

They saw a man wheeling a bulky box from one of the trucks to a door that was propped open at the side of the SeaLife Center.

"I wonder what's in that box," Jess said. "It's enormous."

The man must have had excellent hearing because he turned toward her. "A tank for the new turtle unit," he called.

Jess's eyes lit up. "Turtles, cool!"

"Too bad I won't get to see them," Andi said. "The tanks probably won't be set up until after I go home."

"There'll be plenty to see without turtles," Zack assured her, as they pushed through the doors and entered the SeaLife Center.

Four girls were sitting at a reception desk, dealing with the tickets and programs for the SeaLife Center visitors. A row of turnstiles stood to the left of the desk, and silvery dolphin and whale shapes hung from the ceiling. Attached to one of them was a sign warning visitors that work was being done on security cameras and that there might be some minor disruption to their visit.

A young blond woman with a strong resemblance to Zack waved at them from beside one of the turnstiles. She wasn't wearing the same uniform as the receptionists but was dressed in blue overalls with SEALIFE CENTER printed across one of the pockets. "Hey, Zack!" she called, holding up a set of three tickets and brochures. "Over here!"

Zack introduced his cousin. "Shannon's a water technician," he explained to Jess and Andi. "She regulates the temperatures in the different tanks for all the fish."

"Wow," Andi said, impressed. "That's pretty specialized, huh?"

Shannon grinned. "I help replicate the natural habitats of all the animals at the center," she said. "I love it here. We've got four different sections, all with tanks that need to be kept at different temperatures. See?" She pointed to a large sign.

As Andi started to read it, a cleaner crossed in front of the sign, blocking her view. He was a chubby, red-faced man in gray overalls that had the name of the cleaning company he worked for, Clean-E-Z, embroidered across the back in scarlet letters. Andi was about to step to one side to get a clearer view of the sign when the cleaner moved on across the reception area, pulling his aqua vacuum behind him.

Andi read the sign eagerly, hoping to find out everything she could about the SeaLife Center. There was a cold-water section; a tropical tank for the reef life with an underwater tunnel for viewing; a section for penguins and sea otters; and a section on local marine life, which included dolphins and orcas. Shannon passed her a museum brochure and Andi flipped through it. "Whoa, this place has over eighty thousand fish!"

"We've got a lot to see," Shannon admitted. "Where should we start?"

"You're coming with us?" Zack asked, sounding pleased. "I thought you were working."

Shannon patted a cell phone clipped to her belt. "They'll find me if they need me. Right now, I'm all yours."

"The tropical fish look cool," Jess suggested. "Especially the glass tunnel. Are there any sharks?"

"Yup, we have a couple of reef sharks in there," Shannon said with a smile. "The tropical section is this way."

Glancing at the tanks on either side of them as they followed Shannon, Andi saw lobsters, an octopus, starfish, and a mass of tiny darting blue-and-gold fish, which the brochure said were called Fijian damsels. The dim lighting made Andi feel as if they were underwater, too.

She studied her brochure as they walked down a blue-carpeted corridor patterned in a dolphin motif. The brochure was glossy and gorgeous, the colors of the exotic fish jumping off the page at her. She flipped the leaflet closed. Staring at the beautiful picture of the reef tank on the cover, Andi accidentally bumped into someone coming the other way.

"Oops, sorry!" she apologized, looking up.

A young SeaLife Center employee with blond hair and nice crinkly hazel eyes quickly moved past her. "No problem!" he called over his shoulder, and gave a hurried wave with a dripping hand. Andi was impressed with the way all the employees seemed to take their jobs here so seriously.

She turned the corner then and found herself in front of the tank she'd just seen in the brochure.

"There you are!" Jess exclaimed. "We thought the octopus got you!" She pointed at the wet patches on Andi's shirt. "Maybe we were right."

"Oh." Andi glanced at her damp shirt. "I bumped into a soggy SeaLife Center guy," she explained. Then her eyes widened as she took in the large tank in front of her. It was even more exotic and colorful and busy with reef life than she had expected. "This is fantastic!" she said, moving closer to the glass.

Shannon reeled off the names of some of the fish in

the tank. "We have teardrop butterfly, peacock wrasse, turbo snail," she said, pointing out the fish. Jess and Andi both giggled at the thought of a turbo snail racing along the sandy tank bed.

"They've all got awesome names," Andi said, staring at a group of silvery fish with strong black stripes that Shannon told her were called pajama cardinals.

"Look at these little guys on the tank bed," Zack called from a little farther down the tank. He pointed at a bright yellow fish with pale blue spots, which was sifting busily through the sand.

"Sulphur gobies," said Shannon. "Cute, huh?"

Andi's eye caught a colorful fish she'd noticed on the cover of the SeaLife Center brochure. It was only a couple of inches long and was a very bright orange with beautiful purple fins and four or five black tiger stripes on its body. Swimming beside it were six others. She checked the brochure. "These guys are called flame angels," she announced, glancing up at the tank again. Then, frowning, she looked at the brochure again.

"Shannon?" she said. "When was this picture on the brochure taken?"

Shannon seemed surprised at the question. "Maybe a week before we opened," she said. "Why?"

Andi studied the booklet one more time, then the tank.

The seven flame angels swam together in formation, turning gracefully in a flash of orange and purple before swimming off the other way. "There are eight fish in the picture," she explained, "and I only see seven in the tank."

"The other one's probably hiding," Shannon suggested. "Come on, the glass tunnel is this way. It's a totally wild experience, walking underneath the water!"

Andi followed Shannon, Zack, and Jess down a dimly lit corridor that suddenly burst into pale blue shimmers. She gazed up in amazement, staring at the bellies of the reef fish darting over her head.

"Whoa!" said Zack, craning his neck. "There's a shark!"

A sinewy shape passed overhead with a smooth flick of its tail. Jess shrieked and pulled back with a giggle.

"Hey, Andi. Maybe this shark *ate* the flame angel!" Zack added.

"Not likely." Shannon broke in. "The shark isn't a predator of the fish in this tank. That's why he's here. But the glass tunnel leads from one reef tank to the other," she explained. "Maybe the missing flame angel is on the other side."

The tank on the far side of the tunnel was smaller than the first one. Andi studied the water for a telltale flash of orange and purple, but there was none to be seen.

"Quit looking so worried, Andi," said Jess. "They're tiny fish, and it's a big tank."

A flash of purple and orange appeared from the direction of the glass tunnel. Andi turned to see the troop of flame angels from the first tank swimming gracefully toward her. She counted them again. One, two, three, four, five, six . . . only seven. "Why would seven swim together and one go off on its own?" she asked Shannon. "Is that common for flame angels?"

Shannon shook her head. "I'm not sure," she said, "but I know someone who would be. Hey, Chad!" she called to a dark-haired man who was standing in a corner of the room. "Come here a minute, will you?"

Chad frowned at Andi's question. "I haven't known one flame angel to move away from the others, unless it's sick." He gazed at the fish with a strange expression on his face. "Thanks for noticing," he said at last, turning back to Andi. "We'll check the tank right away. I hope it hasn't died. It would be our first."

A half hour later, Andi sat in the SeaLife Center cafeteria with her friends, prodding at the partly eaten cookie on her plate. She couldn't help thinking about the beautiful little flame angels darting around together in graceful formation. *If the eighth flame angel isn't sick . . .*

"Cheer up, Andi!" Jess poked her in the ribs.

"Yeah, Shannon promised to come tell us when they

find the flame angel," Zack added, slurping noisily at the last of his milk. "Hey, do you want that cookie, Andi? Pecan's my favorite."

"Mine, too," Andi said, swiping the rest of her cookie neatly away from Zack. "You guys, I've been thinking about something. What if the fish—"

Jess gave a fake yawn. "Come on, Detective Andi, this is your vacation! Let's think about something other than fish, okay? Like . . . the mall is open till nine. We could still go bathing suit shopping. Or maybe you want to go blading on the boardwalk this afternoon. We could give Buddy a good run if we were on wheels!"

Andi tried to pull her thoughts back to her friend, who was smiling expectantly at her across the table. "Sure," she said. "That's a great idea."

"Really? Which one?" Jess prompted. "The *shopping*?"

Before Andi could answer, she spotted Shannon hurrying across the cafeteria toward their table.

"I'm glad you're still here," she said, sitting next to Andi. "We can't find the eighth flame angel, and Chad's going crazy."

Andi's heart lurched. "I knew it!" she said. "I got this weird feeling as soon as I saw there were only seven! Are flame angels valuable?"

Shannon nodded. "Sure. You could sell one to a private collector for a nice profit. But I don't understand how a flame angel could have been stolen! You saw Chad in the reef room. SeaLife staff are everywhere!"

"Have you called the police?" Andi asked. "Reported it missing?"

Shannon shook her head. "A missing fish is not exactly a priority during spring break."

Without the police on board, they'd need her help big-time, Andi thought.

Zack's cell phone rang. It was his mom, calling to say that she was waiting for them in the parking lot.

"Thank goodness for that," Jess remarked. "No offense, Shannon, but it's a beautiful day out there and our picnic is calling." She pushed back her chair. "Come on, Andi. Let's go!"

Andi glanced at her friend. Jess was being a great host, planning a ton of activities in Andi's honor and even giving up a shopping trip to visit the SeaLife Center. And Andi *knew* that Jess would be disappointed if she didn't show up to the picnic. . . .

But a missing flame angel was a case for the Pet Finders Club if there ever was one. She couldn't really pass it up just because she was on vacation. . . . Could she?

Chapter Four

Andi held up a hand. "Do you guys mind waiting for just a minute?" she asked her friends. "I really should talk to Shannon about this."

Jess rolled her eyes but stayed where she was.

Relieved, Andi turned back to Shannon. "So, what happens now?" she said. "What's your next step?"

"Chad says we should review the security tapes and check the other tanks as well." Shannon paused, thoughtful. "You know what, maybe we're overreacting. There might be some kind of mix-up we don't know about yet." She smiled at Andi. "You go have fun on the beach," she advised. "There's a new ice-cream stand that just opened on the far side of the marina."

"Gianello's!" Jess said at once. "That's where we went yesterday, Andi. We'll go back there after our picnic."

Jess seemed more than ready to leave. What could

Andi say? "Shannon?" she asked, standing up. "Would you maybe call Zack as soon as you have any news? I'd really like to know if the fish is okay."

Shannon nodded. "Sure," she said with a smile. "Now, go enjoy your vacation!"

Jess steered Andi out of the cafeteria and toward the parking lot. "Vacations are for enjoying. It's just a fish. It's not like an elephant disappeared in Coral Point."

Andi forced herself to smile. It wasn't Jess's fault that she wasn't into pet finding the same way Andi was. "An elephant really would be news," she agreed as she followed her friend into the blazing Florida sunshine.

The evening light lay thick and buttery on the carpeted floor in the Martins' study. Andi stared at the computer screen, wondering what to say in her e-mail to Natalie and Tristan. Was it silly, worrying about a fish? Jess seemed to think so.

"Andi!" Mrs. Martin called down the corridor. "Your mom just called. She'll be over at six o'clock, okay?"

"Sure," Andi replied absently. Composing her thoughts, she turned back to the e-mail.

Hi, guys!
Having an awesome time in the sunshine. I'll have a tan

to drive you crazy when I get home, Nat! We met this cool German shepherd named Laser at the beach yesterday, and the boy in my old house has a cute little Chihuahua, so Buddy hasn't been too lonely! We had a picnic on the beach this afternoon, and Buddy and his new pal fell into a hole some kid dug in the sand. It was pretty funny! ☺

Actually, I wish you guys were here. I think I've got a new case for the Pet Finders Club. A valuable fish has disappeared from the aquarium, and Jess doesn't understand why I can't just forget about it. You would understand though, wouldn't you?

Well, I'll tell you more about the missing fish when I have news. Off to dinner now—just Mom and me. We're going to this taco place down by the marina.

See ya!

Andi

"Finished?" Jess called, peeking into the study. "Jamie and Jonjo are dying for a game of catch before you leave." She tossed a red ball in one hand. "Oh, and we're still going shopping tomorrow, right?"

Feeling oddly guilty for missing her friends back home so much, Andi quickly pressed the SEND button and turned to face Jess. "You bet," she said. "Let's go!"

* * *

Later, in the flickering candlelight at Taco Joe's, Andi talked to her mom about Jess over a huge plate of nachos.

"This sounds awful," she said glumly, "but I keep wishing Tristan and Natalie were here. Does that make me a really bad person, Mom?"

Mrs. Talbot considered the question. "It's natural that you and Jess are developing different interests," she said gently. "You've been apart for a while now, and life in Florida is very different from life in Orchard Park."

"You're telling me!" said Andi with feeling. "I was really disappointed today when Jess didn't care about the missing fish at the SeaLife Center. It seems like all she wants to do is go shopping and impress her new friends."

"That's not true, is it?" Mrs. Talbot said. "You were just telling me earlier what a great time you two are having, doing fun stuff like posing for pictures in the marina, and skating on the boardwalk. It sounds like you've still got plenty in common."

Andi had to admit that her mom was right. "We did have a great time together this afternoon," she said, smiling as she remembered how much Jess had made her laugh by doing an impression of Buddy falling down

the sand hole. They'd seen Jim Harding, the yacht owner, again and had watched Laser spend his whole time chasing seagulls up and down the beach. Jess had done a great impression of that, too.

"There you go!" Mrs. Talbot said.

Andi felt a little bit better. "So," she said between bites of cheese-covered chips, "how are you getting along with Margot? Is it weird spending time with *your* old friend?"

"Kind of," Mrs. Talbot admitted. "She's into this terrible new music that I can't stand. I really hope she doesn't bring it with her when we head south tomorrow."

Andi giggled. Her mom and Margot were about to spend two days in Key West. They'd be back on Thursday morning.

"Before, I would have joked about it with her," Mrs. Talbot continued. "But I haven't said anything this time. It's not really my place anymore. It matters to Margot, so I have to respect that. These are just surface things, Andi. Deep down, where it matters most, our friends are the same as they've always been. We just have to make compromises these days."

Andi took a bite of a taco and considered it. Maybe Mom was right.

*   *   *

On Tuesday morning, Andi awoke to the sound of Jess's cell phone.

"Hey, Zack," Jess said into the receiver. "Are you at your window? I'll just pull back the drapes."

On the far side of Andi's old fence, Zack stood at his window and waved. He flipped his phone shut and shouted across the alley between the two houses. "Shannon called this morning. There's still no sign of that fish. She said Andi wanted to know."

"That's too bad," Jess called back. "Are you still coming to our pool party today?"

"Sure," Zack replied. "I'll see you later!" He closed his window.

Jess turned to Andi. "Let's go to the mall today," she suggested hopefully. "It's our last chance to buy those swimsuits before the party."

Andi really wanted to go back to the aquarium. But she thought about her mom's advice from the night before, about compromising. "Sure," she said. Delight spread across Jess's face. "But," Andi added cautiously, "do you mind if we go back to the SeaLife Center after the mall? I really want to look for clues about the missing fish, Jess. I know pet finding is new to you, but it's important to me."

"No problem," Jess replied. "Mom will want us back

here by one o'clock, though. The party guests are coming at two-thirty, and there's tons of stuff to do before they get here." She started dialing her cell phone. "I'll call Zack back and ask if Shannon can get us in again. Maybe he can meet us there later."

"Deal," Andi agreed. She raised her fist, and Jess tapped it with her own. *Compromising isn't so bad after all,* Andi thought as they grinned at each other.

After a quick breakfast, Mrs. Martin offered to drive the girls to the mall. Andi leaned back in the car and enjoyed the familiar route to their old hangout, passing the SeaLife Center on the way. Jess had arranged for them to meet Zack at eleven. Then Zack's mom would give them a ride home again, in time for the pool party.

"Home, sweet home," Jess gushed, her eyes gleaming as they both stepped into the airy mall and stared around at the stores.

"It's so different," Andi said, trying to recognize a few store names.

"Not all of it." Jess tugged her toward the stairs. "There's a cute bathing suit shop this way, Andi. Hey, maybe we could buy sarongs, too. They're totally in right now. Chloe and Suki always wear them."

An hour later, Andi emerged from the mall with a

bright orange swimsuit patterned in blue and a matching sarong. Jess had chosen a shocking pink suit printed with large yellow flowers, and a pink sarong. Then, to finish the look, she'd persuaded her mom to buy her a floppy pink straw hat as well.

"How do I look?" she said, twirling beside the car with her sun hat pulled down low like a movie star's.

"Totally glam." Andi grinned and hopped into the backseat of Mrs. Martin's car.

They reached the SeaLife Center in ten minutes.

They found Zack sitting on the aquarium steps with a pair of battered sunglasses perched on the end of his nose.

"Looks like your sunglasses caught too many tennis balls yesterday, Zack," Andi joked as they waved good-bye to Jess's mom and headed inside the aquarium.

"Shabby chic is cool, Zack." Jess grinned. "You'll really look the part at our pool party."

Shannon was waiting for them near the reception desk again. "I'll take you straight through to the reef tank," she said, leading the way. "Chad's there."

Sure enough, Chad was in the dimly lit reef room. The bright colors of the reef fish flashed in the tank behind him as they darted and swirled among the rocks and corals. Chad looked gloomy. "I can't understand it," he said. "A fish can't just vanish into thin air."

"Could it have been eaten by a bigger fish?" Zack asked.

"No way!" Chad exclaimed. "Sure, we have some predators here, but we never put them with fish they might prey on."

Andi was glad Zack had asked the question because the thought had been bothering her, too. She hated the idea of one of those beautiful creatures being gobbled up. "I guess fish sometimes die of natural causes," she said.

"Yeah, but we check the tanks all the time and would spot a dead fish right away," Chad assured her.

"Are fish ever taken out of the tanks?" Andi asked. "To be examined or something?" Maybe the missing flame angel had been put back into the wrong tank by mistake.

"They can be," Shannon said. "We had to empty a whole tank once because there was something wrong with the thermostat and the temperature kept changing. But it wasn't this tank."

"I'll check the holding tanks and the register that shows when a fish gets taken out of a tank," Chad said. He headed for a door on the far side of the room. "We have a few tanks out back. I guess it's possible one of the flame angels was taken out by another staff member for some reason. I'll just be two minutes."

Andi scanned the reef tank while she waited for Chad to come back. If only the missing fish had somehow been overlooked. Perhaps it was tucked in behind a coral shelf or concealed in a thick clump of weeds. But there was no sign of it.

Chad reappeared, shaking his head. "All the holding tanks are empty and there's no mention of any flame angels being taken out." He sighed heavily. "So that's that, I guess. It's been stolen."

Although Andi had suspected as much, the announcement still came as a shock.

"Thanks to your observation, Andi," Chad went on, "we have a starting point to work from. According to our security cameras, you came into the reef room at ten-twenty yesterday morning."

Andi remembered the sign that hung in the reception area warning that work was being carried out on security cameras. "Are the cameras working?" she asked eagerly. "Did you see the thief?"

"Unfortunately, no," Chad replied. "Not *all* the cameras are working. Areas where the light is low don't show up at all, so we're gradually replacing the cameras with different models. In this room, there's only one place where a thief could reach into the tank with a net without being picked up by the cameras. By the look of things, this person knew exactly where that was. Whoever it was had certainly done some homework."

"I don't understand why nobody spotted the thief," Andi said. "I mean, there are plenty of staff around. You'd think someone would have spotted a stranger."

"I guess we don't all know each other yet," Shannon explained. "We've only been open a couple of weeks, and loads of different people work here. Some are full-time, but some only come in for a couple of hours a day at busy times. It's pretty likely that we wouldn't spot a stranger."

Andi realized it wasn't going to be easy tracking down the thief with so many staff to interview. *But I'm an experienced pet finder,* she told herself. *And I'll interview a thousand people if it will help me find that flame angel.*

"You can't just take a tropical fish out of a tank and put it in any old container, can you?" she said. "How do you think the thief did it?"

"Very carefully, I hope," Chad replied. "The most important thing is to get the fish used to its new environment. You can't just dump it into another tank. Fish are used to swimming in one particular type of water, and they can react badly if the change is too sudden."

"And changing to a different tank means a whole new balance of minerals and acidity," Shannon added.

"So you gradually get them used to the temperature, then add a little of the new tank water, then a bit more. Sometimes fish go into holding tanks to be sure they're healthy before going into main tanks, so they don't infect other fish if they're sick." She looked very serious for a moment. "Basically," she said at last, "unless the flame angel was stolen by someone who knows a lot about keeping exotic fish, it could be in big trouble."

Andi gulped.

"The other flame angels are over here today, Andi!" Jess called from where she was pressed up close to the glass with Zack. "How many did you see yesterday?"

"Seven," Andi said, joining her friends. She gazed at the bright shoal of fish swooping and gliding through the tank like small multicolored torpedoes. She began to count them: *one, two, three, four, five, six* . . .

Jess turned to Andi. "Do you see what I see?" she asked slowly.

Andi gulped, counting the flame angels again . . . and again. "There are only *six* now!" she cried. "*Another* flame angel has disappeared!"

Chapter Five

"I guess we should leave soon," Andi said, checking her watch. It was almost time for Zack's mom to pick them up. The three of them were standing at one side of the reef room watching Chad and the aquarium security guards making calls about the latest theft.

"But this is just starting to get good!" Jess objected.

Andi turned to her friend. "Getting into pet finding now?" she asked, pleased.

"Well . . ." Jess grinned. "I *was* the one who first noticed that another fish was missing."

Andi linked arms with her friend. "You've got a sharp eye," she told her. "But I think we might be in the way right now. Let's go home and start figuring things out: like who would steal the fish and . . ." She broke off. A fish thief would need a water-filled container to carry the fish away. "The cleaning guy!" she cried. "The one in the reception hall when we first came here."

Jess and Zack stared at her. "What about him?" Zack asked.

"He had a vacuum cleaner with a tank on it. Maybe he had one of the flame angels inside it, and he was only pretending to clean so nobody would suspect him."

Jess's eyes shone. "Wow! We have so got to check this out."

"Come on!" Andi sprinted to the reception area.

There was no sign of the man with the vacuum, so they raced to the desk and waited while the clerk sold tickets to a family with four excited children. "Can you tell me anything about the guy with the vacuum cleaner who was in here yesterday?" Andi asked the clerk when the family had headed for the turnstiles.

The clerk, a slim girl about nineteen years old, looked puzzled. "Harry?" she asked. "Chubby, red-faced guy?"

"That's him."

"What do you want to know?"

"How long has he worked here?"

"Well, he actually works for a contract cleaning firm, so he's not employed by the SeaLife Center. But he's here most days. Nice guy." She broke off to sell a ticket to an elderly lady. "Yesterday, he was amazing. You should have seen what a mess this place was. We had a whole bunch of little kids in and they dropped about a million potato chips just over there." She pointed to the open area where Andi had first seen the cleaning man. "Some of them even spilled their drinks, but Harry wasn't the least bit bothered. He went right to work with his vacuum cleaner, and in about five minutes the place was spotless again."

Andi's high hopes did a nosedive. "Thanks," she said. She moved away from the clerk, and Jess and Zack followed her.

"It couldn't have been him, then," Zack said. "He'd never have used the vacuum cleaner if it had a valuable fish inside."

"What a shame!" Jess sighed. "I really thought we were on to something."

"I guess we'll have to go back to plan A, then," Andi said. "Head home and talk about who else might have stolen the fish, and where they would keep them . . . stuff like that."

"My mom's going to be here any minute," Zack said. "Why don't we take the dogs for a little walk on the beach after we get home? We can talk about it there."

"Good idea," Andi agreed. "My mom always says that

sea air's good for your brain. And don't worry, Jess—"
she smiled at her friend—"we'll be back in time for the
pool party!"

"I wasn't even going to mention it," Jess said sheep-
ishly.

"So," Andi said, watching from the boardwalk as Buddy
hurtled into the waves to fetch Jess's small red rubber
ball. "Where would a thief keep a tropical fish?"

"A home aquarium," Jess suggested. "Or maybe a
pond?"

"Not a pond," said Zack. "These little guys are salt-
water fish, not freshwater fish."

"Good point," Andi said. "So, maybe a home aquarium. I bet there are tons of pet and aquarium stores in
Coral Point, right, Jess?"

"There are a couple on the waterfront," Jess said. "Do
you think the thief might have tried to sell the fish to
them already?"

"Either that or the thief could have bought a home
aquarium recently," Andi said thoughtfully. "They'll need
fish food and other supplies, too. If we talk to all the stores
and put out the word, perhaps we'll trap the thief."

Zack nudged Andi. "Look, there's Mr. Harding," he
said, pointing down the beach.

Andi recognized Jim Harding's burly figure, standing on the beach in his usual white running shorts and blue marina T-shirt. He seemed to be upset about something.

"Laser!" Andi heard Mr. Harding's voice echo across the sand. "Laser!"

"Sounds like Laser might have wandered off," Jess said, jumping down into the sand. "Hey, Mr. Harding! Is everything okay?"

"Have you guys seen Laser anywhere?" Mr. Harding asked, jogging up to them. "He took off down the beach after a seagull this morning and never came back. I've been calling him all morning, and I'm going crazy. What am I going to tell my daughter if I lost him?"

Andi stared at him in dismay. It was now midday. That meant Laser had been missing for hours. No wonder Mr. Harding was so upset!

"That's awful," Jess said, her eyes wide and dark.

"Where have you looked?" Zack asked.

Mr. Harding ran a hand through his thick hair. "I've checked the whole beach at least three times over, and I've asked about him at all the stores. I've stopped pretty much everyone on the boardwalk, too, but no one has seen him. I was getting desperate, so I called the police station as well. Nothing."

Andi pictured the magnificent German shepherd; he was pretty hard to miss. So why hadn't anyone come forward? She pulled her scattered thoughts together. "Did you ask at Gianello's, the ice-cream stand?" she suggested. "He begged for my ice cream there, remember?"

Mr. Harding nodded. "That was the first place I went," he said. "Laser always loves their cones. But they hadn't seen him since yesterday." He passed his hand over his face. "My daughter calls every night to ask if Laser's okay," he muttered. "What am I going to tell her tonight?"

"Is he tagged and collared, Mr. Harding?" Andi asked.

"Yes," he replied, nodding. "If someone finds him, they'll report it, right?"

"I'm sure they will," Andi said as reassuringly as she could. She was about to tell Mr. Harding about her work with the Pet Finders Club when she stopped herself. What would Jess say about looking for *another* animal during their vacation?

Jess answered Andi's question for her. "Mr. Harding, Andi's an expert pet finder," she announced. "She does it all the time back home. She's been in the papers and everything. There's nothing she can't find." She looked hopefully at Andi. "Right?"

"Right." Andi nodded. "I've solved a bunch of cases with my friends back in Orchard Park," she said. "We can help you if you want."

Jim Harding looked so relieved that for a moment, Andi thought he was going to cry. "Thanks," he said at last. "I need all the help I can get."

Andi kicked into pet-finding mode. "Tell us again," she said, pulling a notebook and pen out of her backpack. "When did you last see Laser?"

"About eight a.m.," Mr. Harding said slowly, then he steadily went through the rest of the details so that Andi could write it all down.

"You should keep checking the beach," Andi advised, putting her pen and notebook away. "Zack, why don't you go with Mr. Harding. Jess and I will check in the opposite direction. That way, we cover twice the distance—and the chance of missing Laser along the way is halved."

Jim Harding nodded. "Good idea. Let's meet at Gianello's ice-cream stand in an hour."

Jess set off toward the marina with a determined expression on her face as Mr. Harding, Zack, and Huck jogged away from them. Andi whistled for Buddy and then ran after her friend.

"Hey, Jess," Andi began, "I just wanted to say thanks.

You know, for offering to help Mr. Harding find Laser. I know it's not your ideal vacation, but—"

"Don't worry about it," Jess interrupted, looking a little embarrassed. "It's only twelve-thirty now. We can search the beach and still get back home in time to set up for the pool party. Just think how cool it would be if we did find Laser!"

Andi smiled. Jess was as good a friend as she'd always been.

Jess winked. "We'll be heroes. And Chloe and Suki will be totally impressed!" She began calling for the dog. "Here, Laser! Here, boy!"

Andi laughed and shook her head. *So maybe Jess's eagerness isn't exactly for the right reasons,* she said to herself. *But at least it's a start!*

At three o'clock, Andi was lying on a sun lounger at Jess's poolside. Her new swimsuit had gotten lots of compliments, but she was finding it hard to get into the party. Andi, Jess, Zack, and Mr. Harding hadn't found Laser, although they had looked for over an hour, and Andi's voice was hoarse from calling the dog and asking questions on the boardwalk. She stared at the plate of sandwiches beside her lounge chair. She wasn't feeling hungry.

Music thumped cheerfully from the speakers on the Martins' back porch, sometimes loud and sometimes soft, as Jess's little brothers, Jonjo and Jamie, kept fiddling with the volume and running away with a giggle. Jess had been right—lots of people had come. Andi recognized most of them, and it had been kind of fun talking about her old school and all the stuff that had changed since Andi had gone away. Then Suki and Chloe had arrived—fashionably late, of course—wearing identical bright blue swimsuits and enormous sunglasses. It'd been impossible to catch Jess's attention since, even though Andi was dying to talk to her about Laser.

"What's up, Andi?" Zack asked from behind her.

"Hey, Zack," she said, turning to face him. "Having a good time?"

Zack perched on the edge of her lawn chair. "Sure," he said. "Mrs. Martin makes a mean salsa. Did you try it yet?"

Andi prodded at her sandwiches. Buddy, lying in the shade beneath her table, sniffed hopefully at the plate and then settled back down again with his head between his paws. "I'm not very hungry," she confessed. "I keep thinking about poor Laser, lost on the beach." She reached down and stroked Buddy's head. "I lost Buddy once, right after we moved to Orchard Park. I thought I would go crazy, worrying about him."

"I know what you mean," Zack admitted. "It seems wrong somehow, sitting around here and enjoying ourselves when we don't know where Laser is."

"Who's Laser?" asked a girl with freckles and a cute straw hat on her head. She was sitting on the chair beside Andi's. "I'm Holly, by the way."

"A friend's dog has disappeared," Andi explained. "We were out looking for him all morning."

"Too bad," said the girl, her eyes bright with sympathy. "What kind of dog?"

"A German shepherd."

"Who's got a German shepherd?" asked a tall boy who Andi recognized as David, formerly the smallest kid in her class. "German shepherds are the best. My stepfather has one."

Andi explained again about Laser. Soon, there was a group of kids clustered around her and Zack, all wanting to know more about what had happened.

"He was chasing seagulls, you said? My mom's poodle does that."

"What are you going to do next?" Holly asked.

"Back home, my friends and I started a group called the Pet Finders Club," Andi told her. "We work

together and search for clues, ask people questions . . . stuff like that. We've found dozens of missing
pets that way," she said. "So we'll probably do that here,
too."

The idea of a Pet Finders Club seemed to interest the
group of partygoers even more than the story of Laser.
Soon they were all discussing what they might be able
to do to help.

"Andi?" Jess came over to Andi's chair.

"Hey!" Andi said. "Can you believe how much everyone wants to help find Laser?" She gestured happily to
the chattering group. "They can't stop talking about it!"

Jess leaned in close. "Can you lighten up on the
pet-finding stuff already?" she asked in a whisper, then
glanced back over her shoulder.

Following her friend's gaze, Andi noticed Chloe and
Suki sitting alone on the far side of the pool. They were
both wearing that sour look on their faces—the one
that Andi remembered.

"Chloe and Suki are getting bored," Jess whispered.
"No one's talking to them. Everyone's over here."

"They're welcome to come over and join in," Zack
suggested.

"No way." Jess looked tense. "They don't want to talk
about missing pets at a pool party."

"Then tell them they can leave," someone said from behind Andi's chair.

"Uh-oh," Andi murmured to Zack. "I think they heard that."

"Yup," Zack said. "They're coming over."

The group parted as the two blond girls approached them.

"No problem!" Chloe said, looking furious.

"None!" Suki added.

Chloe turned to Jess. "This is the lamest party I've ever been to," she said, folding her arms across her chest. "Come on, Suki. Let's go over to your place. At least we'll have some fun *there*."

"Yeah!" Suki said, shooting a poisonous look at Jess. "No pets missing there."

The color drained from Jess's face as the two girls stomped away and disappeared out the backyard gate. Andi felt awful.

"Oh, Jess!" she said, jumping up out of her seat. "I'm so sorry! I know how much you wanted to impress Chloe and Suki. I didn't mean—"

"Forget it," Jess said in a tight voice. She looked as if she were about to cry. "They're wrong. I mean, Laser can't help it if he's missing."

There were fierce murmurs of agreement all around Jess.

"They *were* pretty mean about it," Andi admitted.

"If it helps, Jess," Holly spoke up, "this is the best pool party I've ever been to. Really!"

There were more shouts of agreement.

Jess gave a watery smile. "Thanks, guys." She paused. "Hey, I've got an idea. Why don't we move the party to the beach? That way, we can look for Laser and still have fun. Mom will keep the food in the refrigerator for later."

Several kids cheered—and one of them was Andi.

"No way are Chloe and Suki the coolest girls at your school, Jess," Andi said, hooking an arm around her friend's shoulders. "That honor totally goes to you."

Chapter Six

Fifteen minutes later, Andi and Jess and Zack had organized everyone into three groups, covering the beach, the marina, and the waterfront stores. Andi whipped out her digital camera, showing everybody the picture she had taken of Laser the other day. She noted the German shepherd's distinct coloring on his paws before sending the groups on the search. They all agreed to meet back at Gianello's in an hour.

Just as Andi had hoped, there were hundreds of people on the beach that afternoon. The kids stopped and asked as many people as they could if they'd seen a young German shepherd anytime that day. "He has three black paws and a copper one. . . ." "He's around two years old. . . ." "Yes, on his own . . ." Andi found herself describing Laser so many times that she could almost picture him sniffing around at her feet. Buddy raced around the beach, sensing the excitement of the hunt.

Jess's group jogged up breathlessly to Gianello's an hour later. "We got a couple of maybes, but then we found the dogs and they were with their owners all along."

"Nothing from the store owners," Zack reported. "Sorry."

"Nothing for us, either," Andi said with a sigh.

"So what do we do now, Andi?" a girl in Zack's group asked her.

Andi gulped as everyone stared at her expectantly. She wasn't sure what to do next. They didn't have a single clue about the missing dog—just that he had disappeared around eight o'clock that morning. What *could* they do? "Let's go back to Jess's place," she said at last. "We could probably use some food, right?"

"And a swim," suggested a short boy with glasses. "I'm sweating!"

"We'll figure out the next part of our plan on the way back," Jess said, linking arms with Andi.

The next part of our plan, Andi thought. *Come on, Andi—think!* This vacation was turning her brain to sand. Glancing at Jess chattering happily with Holly on her left, she gave herself a mental shake. Jess had been brave enough to deal with Chloe and Suki's rejection.

Now it was up to Andi to pull herself together and turn up the heat on their hunt for Laser. But how?

Back at Jess's place, the party guests gathered around the food by the poolside. With some chips in her hand and Buddy's comforting presence beneath her chair, Andi focused her mind. She had to get back to basics.

"Posters!" she said triumphantly. "We always make posters back home when pets disappear. I can use the picture I took of Laser! We could print them on your computer, Jess, and then put them up along the waterfront."

"Sounds good," said Jess before diving neatly into the deep end.

David popped his head out of the pool and rested his chin on the poolside. "Small problem," he said, squinting up at Andi. "Where do we put posters? There aren't many trees along the boardwalk."

Andi frowned. "Maybe flyers instead?" she said. "We can hand them out to people."

"Hey!" Holly said excitedly as she jumped out of the pool. "What about putting Laser's picture on sandwich boards and walking around the beach wearing them? We're sure to grab attention that way!"

"Genius!" Andi cried. She made a mental note to consider sandwich boards next time they were looking for missing pets back home. "I can go get the picture printed and blown up this afternoon. There must be a store in town where they can do that quickly, right?"

"Next to the marina," said Holly, nodding.

"We've got plenty of big cardboard boxes in our garage to make sandwich boards with." Jess climbed out of the pool, her eyes alight with the challenge.

Jess's mom found some large sheets of paper, and Andi organized the guests into groups: some to make the sandwich boards and others to draw up posters with bright markers, leaving a space for Laser's photo in the center. Andi quickly wriggled into some clothes and grabbed her camera, and Holly agreed to take her to the photo shop.

"You'd better hurry!" Jess called as Andi and Holly pulled on their shoes. "It's already five-thirty, and the store closes in half an hour!"

Andi felt like she'd never run so fast in her life. Fortunately, Holly was almost as fast as she was and they reached the store in ten minutes flat. Twenty minutes later they emerged, carefully carrying two stacks of pictures between them.

"He's a really pretty dog," Holly said as they walked back to Jess's house. "He looks so smart, too. I'm sure he's going to be fine."

Andi looked at the photograph. Laser seemed to smile

out at the world, his pink tongue lolling in the heat and his coat shining like ebony. She felt a fresh wave of determination wash over her.

Zack was finishing the second sandwich board as Andi and Holly walked back through the house. Both boards looked fantastic. The teams had been hard at work writing LASER VANISHES! and HAVE YOU SEEN THIS DOG? in huge red letters at the top and bottom of their sheets of paper, which were now stuck neatly on the sandwich boards. Two perfect-sized spaces sat in the middle of the boards, waiting for the photographs.

Jess passed the glue over, and Andi and Holly carefully pasted the photographs in place.

"Wow!" Andi said, standing back to admire the effect. "People will be able to see Laser's face for miles!"

"We can take the boards straight down to the beach," Jess began.

"Kids!" Mrs. Martin stood at the porch door beside a very tall man with a shock of black hair. "You'll have to take your sandwich boards to the beach tomorrow. David's dad is here. And so are Holly's and Sharon's."

A groan of disappointment went up around the pool. It looked as if the party was over.

Soon more parents arrived to take Jess's friends home. The guests left reluctantly, after making Andi and

Jess promise to pass on news about Laser as soon as they heard anything.

"I really meant it when I said this was the best pool party I've ever been to," Holly said, hugging both Jess and Andi. "I hope you find Laser soon. And don't worry about Chloe and Suki, Jess. They just couldn't deal with Laser getting all the attention."

After the last guests had left, Zack and Andi and Jess helped Mrs. Martin tidy the mess, and Jonjo and Jamie propped up the sandwich boards on the back porch.

"You know what?" Jess stopped wiping down the picnic table and turned to Andi. "I really don't mind about Chloe and Suki. I thought I would, but I don't."

"Good for you!" Andi said and squeezed her friend's arm.

"Their swimsuits were cute, though, weren't they?" Jess said wistfully. "I kind of wish I'd bought a blue one now." Andi couldn't help laughing.

That evening, Andi checked her e-mail to find a message from Tristan waiting for her.

Hey, Andi!
Totally jealous about the Florida weather and the fish hunting. Nat and I did some research when we got your e-mail.

We did an Internet search for fish enthusiasts—thought there were bound to be some fish blogs out there. Anyway, we found the Web site of a crazy tropical fish guy. And guess what? He lives in Coral Point! Coincidence? Seriously, you should check him out: www.larrytjhook. If he's not your thief, then he'll have plenty of advice for you, at least. A fish guy named Hook! *Get it?*

With the whole Laser case going on, Andi had almost forgotten about the flame angels! She typed a reply:

Thanks for the fish info. I'll check it out right away. You won't believe it, but we have another *case now. Remember Laser, the German shepherd I told you about? He's missing! Jess had a pool party this afternoon and we organized everyone to ask questions at the beach and make sandwich boards with Laser's picture on it. We worked really hard, but we didn't get any answers. We're taking the boards down to wear around the beach tomorrow, to see if we have any more luck.*

Thoughtfully, Andi signed off. Then she typed *www. larrytjhook.com* into Jess's computer and clicked SEARCH.

A bright Web site popped onto the screen with animated fish swimming endlessly along the bottom of the picture. It looked like a blog with pictures and general advice about keeping tropical fish tanks. As Andi stared at the latest entry, her heart began to race.

"What's up?" Jess came into the study and sat down next to Andi at the computer.

Andi showed her.

"You're back on the fish?" Jess asked with surprise. "I thought now we were looking for Laser—"

"Don't worry. We can run two cases at the same time," Andi assured her. "Look, read what this guy says about how he's gotten a new delivery of fish. He doesn't mention the breed, but don't you think he sounds kind of secretive?"

" *'Just got some troptastic new babies in,'* " Jess read aloud. " *'They're adjusting to their new home, so I won't upload any photos until they're settled. But watch this space! They'll blow your mind!'* " Jess looked up at Andi, her eyes wide. "You think he means the flame angels?"

Andi made a decision. "I'm going to send him an e-mail."

"But if he's the thief, you'll scare him off!" Jess objected as Andi started typing.

"Don't worry," said Andi, frowning with concentration.

"I'll pretend to be doing a school project on tropical fish tanks. I'll ask if we can go see him and talk about it."

"We can't go visit some strange fish thief," Jess began.

"We won't go on our own," Andi said. "My friends and I did that once before, back in Orchard Park, and ended up in a creepy old house. It was dangerous. No way am I doing that again. If this Larry Hook guy says yes, we can take an adult with us." She finished typing the e-mail, clicked SEND, and sat back.

"Now what?" Jess sounded nervous as she watched the e-mail disappear from the screen.

"Now," Andi said, "we wait."

The next morning Andi and Jess hurried eagerly into the study to check for e-mail. But Andi's inbox was empty.

"Never mind," Jess consoled her over a breakfast of melon and cereal on the Martins' sunny back porch. "Let's go find Zack and then take the sandwich boards to the beach."

After a quick call to her mom down in Key West, Andi stuffed her beach things into her bag and whistled for Buddy. The little terrier bounded out into the garden with his tail wagging itself into a blur.

"Time for the beach, Bud!" Andi fussed over Buddy,

who promptly rolled over and showed off his plump white tummy. "And I need you to put your best sniffing nose on, too. We're looking for Laser again today."

Buddy pricked up his ears and looked alert. Jess laughed. "I swear that dog understands everything we say!"

"He does!" Andi joked, and Buddy barked twice. "See?" she added.

The girls tucked the sandwich boards under their arms and waved good-bye to Mrs. Martin and Jess's little brothers. Then they jogged around to Zack's house.

Zack flung open the door just as Andi was about to ring the bell. "I was about to call you guys!"

"Great minds think alike," Andi said with a grin. She handed over her sandwich board. "Take this, will you? I'm having a little difficulty holding that *and* Buddy."

As if to prove her point, Buddy barked and started running around Andi's legs, tangling himself up with his leash.

Zack took the board. "I think I'll leave Huck at home today," he said, pulling the door behind him. "The poor guy is still snoozing underneath our kitchen table."

"Come on, guys," Jess insisted, already out on the sidewalk. "The sooner we get down to the beach, the sooner we'll find Laser!"

The sun was already hot, even though it was early, and the beach was filling up. Andi and Zack both put on the sandwich boards, while Jess took charge of Buddy and a notebook, where they planned to record any clues they found.

After around half an hour, Andi and Jess got their first reaction.

"Whoa, those boards look righteous," said a friendly surfer with a petite girlfriend whose long dark hair fell almost to her waist. "I saw a German shepherd early yesterday morning. It looked like that dog." He pointed to Laser's picture.

"Great!" Andi cried as Jess scribbled furiously in the notebook. "Can you remember what time it was?"

The man glanced at his girlfriend. "Uhhh . . . around eight or nine?" he said. "It was a little earlier than today."

Eight o'clock fit exactly with the last time Jim Harding had seen Laser! "Was the dog with anybody?" Andi asked hopefully.

"Some guy," the dark-haired girl chimed in. "He was running along the boardwalk with the dog. He was around fifty years old, I'd say. Brown hair. Oh, and he was wearing a blue marina T-shirt."

Andi's heart sank. The girl had just described Jim Harding!

The girl turned to her boyfriend with a frown. "Hey, are you sure it was yesterday morning?" she asked. "Wasn't it the day before yesterday?"

The surfer reconsidered. "Maybe it was two days ago," he confessed. "Sorry. We're on vacation. The days kind of blend together."

"That's too bad," Jess said, putting the lid back on her pen. "Thanks, anyway."

Andi controlled her disappointment as best she could and thanked the couple. "I thought we had a real clue there for a minute," she said as the couple walked away.

"Hey, guys!" Zack called from down the beach. "This lady says she saw a German shepherd about nine o'clock yesterday morning!" He shifted his sandwich board to a more comfortable position and struggled through the soft sand toward Andi and Jess. "She says he was alone and sniffing around some towels on the beach," he panted, finally reaching them. "She doesn't like dogs much; she avoided him because he wasn't on a leash."

"Did she see where he went?" Andi asked.

"Toward the marina," Zack replied.

"So what are we waiting for?" Andi said with excitement. "Let's go!"

Their sandwich boards attracted a great deal of attention as they hurried side by side along the boardwalk toward the marina. Jess darted through the crowd, asking questions and pointing at the boards. Everyone seemed interested, but no one had anything more to add.

"We should check out Mr. Harding's boat, the *Happy Jack*," Andi suggested when they arrived at the marina. "Maybe Laser got lost and tried to find Mr. Harding over there."

"Let's ask that guy at the refreshment stand where the *Happy Jack* is moored." Zack pointed to a teenager with long sandy hair and a red baseball cap perched on the back of his head. He stood behind a cart filled with drinks and snacks.

The young man recognized the photographs of Laser immediately.

"Laser's a great dog," he said, leaning over his stand to take a closer look at Andi's sandwich board. "He likes to beg for burgers. Mr. Harding had to drag him away from my stand three times last week."

"Sounds right." Andi grinned, remembering how Laser had begged for her ice-cream cone. "He ran off at around eight o'clock yesterday morning, and we wondered if maybe he'd headed for the *Happy Jack*. Do you know where it's docked?"

The refreshment-stand guy started to give them directions—and then stopped. "Eight o'clock yesterday morning, you said?" he asked. "Are you sure? I saw Laser and Mr. Harding running together on the far side of the marina at around ten yesterday."

Andi frowned. That didn't make sense. "Mr. Harding definitely told us that he'd lost Laser around eight o'clock."

The young man shrugged. "Just telling you what I saw," he said.

"Do you think maybe you could be confused?" Zack asked.

The teenager took off his red cap and scratched his head. "Nope. I don't start work on the stand until nine-thirty," he said. "Anyway, the *Happy Jack*'s moored about ten boats along that last pontoon over there. I'm Ben," he said. "Let me know if I can help any more. I sure hope you find Laser soon."

"That is so weird," Jess muttered as they walked slowly away from the refreshment stand toward where the *Happy Jack* was moored. "Why would Mr. Harding lie about when he lost Laser?"

Andi's head whirled. Jess was right—it *was* weird. *Too* weird.

Chapter Seven

As Andi, Jess, and Zack traveled down the final pontoon in search of the *Happy Jack,* they saw a familiar figure jogging along the silvery boards toward them.

"Hey there!" Jim Harding cried, coming to a stop beside them. "I've been down on the beach this morning, asking about Laser. It seems everyone knows about him already! You kids have been pretty busy."

Andi glanced down at her board. "These are kind of hard to miss," she said. "We were asking around yesterday, too, with a bunch of friends." She squinted at the man, trying to figure out a good way to ask him again when he'd lost Laser without seeming as though she were doubting him. "So, um, *when* did you say you last saw Laser, again?"

"Around eight o'clock," Mr. Harding replied. "He's been missing for over twenty-four hours now. My daughter was very upset about it last night." He summoned a smile as he looked at Andi's and Zack's sandwich boards. "Look, I really appreciate what you kids are doing," he said. "We're sure to find him before too long."

Andi *wanted* to believe Mr. Harding. She glanced at Zack and Jess. But Ben had seemed so sure of himself. . . . None of it made any sense. Why would either of them lie?

With a shake of her head, Andi pulled her thoughts back to the *Happy Jack*. "A woman Zack spoke to thinks she saw Laser heading for the marina yesterday morning," she told Mr. Harding. "We thought we'd check out the *Happy Jack*—just in case he was hiding belowdeck or something."

"I just came from there," Mr. Harding said. "I had the same thought. Laser loves sleeping on the boat. Still, you're welcome to take another look."

"Maybe we should." Andi took off her sandwich board and placed it neatly on the pontoon, then took Buddy's leash from Jess. "Come on, Bud. Time to get that nose into action."

Buddy trotted happily along the pontoon, sniffing at each boat they passed. The *Happy Jack* was white with maroon waves painted along its sides. It looked a little scuffed, but the deck shined and the chrome rails gleamed in the bright morning sunshine. Andi watched Buddy carefully as he sniffed around the sloop's little deck—but to her disappointment, Buddy didn't seem to pick up Laser's scent anywhere.

Another dead end, she thought in frustration.

"Well, I've got to get to work," Jim Harding said, interrupting Andi's train of thought. "You know where my store is, right? It's the yachting goods place off the boardwalk."

Zack and Jess nodded as Andi pulled her sandwich board back on.

"If you hear anything, come find me!" said Mr. Harding, settling his sunglasses back on his nose before he jogged away.

"You're very quiet, Andi," Zack commented.

"Just thinking," Andi murmured, staring after the man.

"Well, let's think about what we're going to do next," Jess suggested. "How about asking around the boats, since we're here at the marina?"

They agreed to split the pontoons between them. There were fifteen of them across the marina, which meant they could take five each. Then they agreed to walk around the perimeter of the marina together before they left.

Andi worked her way down her five pontoons with surprising speed, Buddy trotting obediently at her side. There weren't many boats in the harbor that morning—most of them seemed to have sailed off for the day. It wasn't surprising. There were plenty of beautiful islands off the Florida coast. If she had a boat, she'd sail it every day she could.

A few people tinkered on their boats in the calm sunshine of the morning—several of them recognized Laser, but no one had seen him the day before. Andi hoped that her friends were having better luck and jogged down to the marina perimeter to find them.

Zack and Jess were both waiting for her beside a familiar-looking boat. Andi recognized it at once. It was the *Lemming*—the glamorous cruiser with the even more glamorous owners—where they'd embarrassed themselves by doing silly poses over the weekend. She felt herself blush at the memory.

"We can't ask here!" Jess whispered, trying to drag Andi and Zack farther down the edge of the marina.

Andi looked surprised. "I know, but what if they saw something?"

"No way. Let's skip this one and go to the next boat." Jess tugged at Zack's sleeve, trying to move him down the marina as quickly as she could. Jess turned bright red when Buddy tugged away from Andi and ran barking up the gangplank of the *Lemming*.

"Buddy!" Andi called, wriggling out of her board and laying it on the ground. "Come back!" She heard an answering bark from somewhere deep inside the *Lemming*.

"The photographers and his model return!" a man called.

Suddenly feeling self-conscious, Andi turned to see the tanned young boat owner smiling at her from the deck of the *Lemming*. *Caught!*

"So, how did the pictures come out?" the owner asked, setting down the armful of boxes he'd been carrying. "You guys looked like you were having a lot of fun."

"We haven't printed them yet," Andi mumbled, then changed the subject. "Listen, I'm really sorry, but my dog just ran onto your boat. Do you mind if I come up and get him?"

"Be my guest." The man squinted down at Zack, who was still wearing his sandwich board. "That's a familiar-looking dog," he said. "We've seen him around the marina. Is he lost?"

"He disappeared yesterday morning," Andi explained. "Have you seen him?" she added hopefully.

The boat owner shook his head. "Not in the past couple days," he said. He extended his hand. "I'm Carl Lem, by the way. Welcome aboard the *Lemming*."

The red-haired woman Andi remembered seeing on the *Lemming*'s deck suddenly emerged from the boat's dark wooden interior, holding a wriggling bundle of tan-and-white fur. "Is this what you're looking for?" she asked.

Andi stretched out her arms gratefully and took Buddy, who promptly licked her chin. "Sorry," she said. "He doesn't usually do stuff like this."

Carl Lem introduced the red-headed woman as Sara, his wife. "We just got married last week," he said, putting his arm around his wife's waist. "We're about to head out for a three-week honeymoon cruise to the islands," he explained, "and we've been stocking up on food and supplies." He winked. "I guess your dog smelled the steak in that box over there."

Andi grinned. "Steak is Buddy's favorite," she said, holding on tightly to Buddy, who was sniffing and straining in her arms. "I'm Andi. And down there are my friends Jess and Zack."

Jess and Zack waved from the pontoon below.

"Sorry about the missing dog," Sara Lem said as Andi walked back down the gangplank and set Buddy down, taking care to wrap his leash tightly around her hand.

"We'll ask around the yachting club before we leave," Carl Lem offered. "Do you have a number we can call if we hear anything?"

"They were nice after all," Jess said as they waved good-bye and headed farther down the edge of the marina. "Too bad they couldn't tell us anything about Laser."

"The main thing is that we're following up the clue about Laser being at the marina," Andi said, shoulder-ing her sandwich board again. "If we keep it up, *some-one's* bound to know something. I mean, a dog can't just disappear into thin air."

Zack pulled a face. "What with the flame angels and now Laser, I'm starting to think they should rename this place Vanishing Point instead of Coral Point."

Jess nodded glumly. Noticing Andi's blank look, she explained, "When you're sailing, the vanishing point is when a ship disappears on the horizon."

Andi nodded. Zack was right—this place *was* turning into a vanishing point, but it wasn't just ships sailing over the horizon. Fish and dogs were vanishing, too!

Andi's cell phone jingled from somewhere deep in her pocket. Wriggling around inside her sandwich board as best she could, she managed to pull it out.

"Who's calling?" Zack asked, peering over Andi's shoulder.

Andi frowned. "I don't recognize the number," she said. She clicked it on. "Hello?"

"Is this Andi Talbot?" asked a gravelly voice. "This is Larry Hook. You e-mailed me about your reef aquarium project yesterday?"

Andi's heart jumped. She squeezed the phone tightly to her ear and motioned furiously at Jess to pull out her notebook. "Hello, Mr. Hook! Thanks for calling!"

Zack looked a little confused, and Andi realized that they hadn't filled him in on the Web site they'd found. She left Jess to explain and turned back to her conversation.

"No problem," Mr. Hook was saying. "Any particular fish you're interested in?"

Andi thought as fast as she could. If Larry Hook was the fish thief, she didn't want to give him any kind of warning about the flame angels. "Um, reef dwellers," she said, a little lamely. "Small ones, mostly. The kind that swim around in shoals?"

"I have plenty of those," Mr. Hook said. "Why don't you come over and take a look for yourself? It'll be easier to answer your questions if we have the fish right in front of us."

Andi repeated the address to Jess, who scribbled it in the notebook. "Thanks, Mr. Hook," she said at last.

"We'll see you later. Two o'clock." Her heart pounded as she clicked off the phone and turned to her friends. "He's asked us over this afternoon! Sunset Place is just a couple blocks from where you live, Jess. Do you think your mom or dad could come with us?"

"I guess we could ask my dad to take us," Jess replied. "He's got the afternoon off today. But what about Laser?" she asked with a frown. "Isn't he more important than some fish?"

Andi understood how Jess was feeling, but she also knew that *both* cases were important—even if a fish couldn't give you cuddly hugs and friendly slurps on your face. "It'll only take an hour," she said.

Paul Martin, Jess's dad, was happy to accompany Jess, Andi, and Zack that afternoon. Andi left Buddy to play with Jonjo and Jamie, then ran out to join Jess and the others as they made their way down the street toward Sunset Place.

"I think I've heard of this guy," Mr. Martin said, following them down the driveway and onto the sidewalk. "He has a column in the local paper." He smiled around at them all. "I'm really impressed that one visit to the SeaLife Center has got you all interested in fish."

Jess winked at Andi. They'd told Mr. Martin that they

had developed a sudden interest in marine life. *Which is true,* Andi thought. It was just that they were interested in two fish in particular—the missing flame angels.

"Maybe he's not the thief after all," Jess whispered to Andi as they headed down the street.

Andi had a feeling that maybe Jess was right. It seemed unlikely that someone who wrote for a local newspaper would be a thief. "Well," she said, "it's the only clue we've got on the flame angels right now. Even if he doesn't have the fish, I'm sure he'll have *something* he can tell us. I mean, he's a tropical fish expert. That has to be useful, right?"

Larry Hook was a large bear of a man, with a thick brown beard and a round stomach that was wrapped a little too tightly in a black T-shirt. "Great to see you!" he said, shaking hands enthusiastically with everyone and standing aside to let them through his front door. "The tanks are out at the back. I built a special extension to my house for my collection. Humidity, temperature, light—they're all really important for the fish."

Andi blinked as they stepped out from the dark hall into a large white room set with skylights. She counted six different tanks, ranging from a small one to the left of the door to an enormous one that took up the entire back wall. Fish of every color and size swam lazily around her in their cool blue tanks, making Andi feel as if she was swimming alongside them.

"They're all reef fish," Mr. Hook explained, "but some are a little more sociable than others." He gestured to a large tank over to the right. A long, spotted, snakelike fish was resting quietly on the bottom. "Leopard moray eel," he explained. "A predator who doesn't care for company."

Andi remembered that she was supposed to be here for a school project. She dug a notebook out of her pocket and prepared to write notes. "It's a very big tank for just one fish," she said.

"Don't be fooled," said Larry Hook. "This little fellow's young. Leopard morays can grow up to six feet long."

Jess shuddered. "Do they bite?" she asked.

"Sure," Mr. Hook said with a grin. "But they won't kill you. That little guy, on the other hand, is pretty poisonous." He indicated the small tank that Andi had noticed by the door. It contained an extraordinary spiky-looking fish with dramatic brown-and-cream coloring that Andi recognized from the SeaLife Center.

"A lionfish, right?" she said, staring with fascination at the creature swimming grandly from side to side in its tank.

"You've been doing your homework," Mr. Hook said

approvingly. "That's right. They have poisonous sting-ers in their dorsal fins that can pack a punch."

"Do you have any, uh, *friendly* fish, Mr. Hook?" Zack asked.

Larry Hook threw back his head and laughed. His belly wobbled. "Plenty," he said at last. "Over there!"

He indicated two tanks. One was the large tank that covered the back wall, containing shoals of brightly colored fish. The other, at first glance, appeared to be empty. Andi moved in for a closer look.

Swimming delicately among the waving seaweed on the tank bed, two little sea horses came into view. They moved with a gentle rocking motion, their noble horse-shaped heads held up high and their tails curling and uncurling beneath them.

"Sea horses!" Jess gasped, pressing close to the glass. "I love these fish! They're amazing!"

Andi moved to the large tank and peered in at the colorful residents that darted up and down and side to side as she watched.

Mr. Hook reeled off a series of names. "Blue damsels, peacock wrasse, scooter blenny . . . This is what I call my rainbow tank, because of all the colors."

"Do you have any flame angels, Mr. Hook?" Andi asked cautiously.

"Centropyge loriculus," Larry Hook responded promptly. "Not yet, but I hope to acquire some shortly. The wild-caught ones are the best, although the tank-bred variety is much cheaper. They're beautiful, aren't they? Their colors are unreal."

"Your blog said that you'd recently gotten some new fish," Jess said boldly. "What kind did you get?"

Andi held her breath in anticipation.

"Two queen triggers!" Mr. Hook announced, dashing Andi's hopes. "I have them in an isolation tank over here."

The queen triggers were spectacular. Colored vivid yellow, blue, and turquoise, they had chunky bodies with royal blue fins positioned right next to their flowing tails.

"They're pretty mean, but they're worth it," Mr. Hook remarked with a broad grin. "Beauties, aren't they?"

"Where do you get your fish?" Zack asked.

"I use specialist suppliers all over the States," Mr. Hook replied. "But there are plenty of terrific stores in town that can usually supply some rare and exotic breeds. They mostly sell their stock to the tourist trade that wants reef fish as a reminder of happy vacations in the Sunshine State."

"Aren't fish a little fragile to be sold to tourists?" Andi wanted to know.

"Most of them are responsible stores," Mr. Hook told her. "They sell their fish with clear instructions about acclimatization and quarantine."

Andi wrote thoughtfully in her notebook: CHECK OUT PHONE BOOK FOR FISH STORES. "Thanks for your time, Mr. Hook," she said at last, closing her notebook and putting it in her bag. "You've been really helpful."

"Good luck with the assignment," the fish expert replied, leading them back to the front door and shaking hands with them all. "Fingers crossed for an A, right?"

"We didn't get much there, did we?" Zack said gloomily as they followed Mr. Martin down the path to the street.

"Not much," Andi admitted. "Sorry to drag you out there, Jess," she said, turning apologetically to her friend.

"That's okay," Jess said. She looked surprisingly enthusiastic. "Mr. Hook's sea horses were so cool! Dad thought so, too. Right, Dad?"

"Pretty impressive," Mr. Martin admitted.

"I think we should buy some," Jess said, slipping her hand onto her dad's arm. "Can we go check out a pet store, Dad? Please?"

Mr. Martin frowned. "I don't know. Sea horses take a lot of looking after, since they're more delicate than most fish. But I guess we can look into it. There's a store called Fin Fun not far from the waterfront," he said. "They have the best range of fish in town. If anyone has sea horses, they will. But, Jess—"

"I know, I know, you can't promise anything," Jess interrupted. "You and Mom always said no pets, but sea horses don't really count, do they? They're so quiet!" She turned and winked at Andi. "Can you imagine Chloe's and Suki's faces when they hear I have *sea horses*?"

Andi stared at her, surprised that her friend still cared what those two thought.

Jess pointed both index fingers at Andi. "Gotcha! You should have seen your face!"

"You got me, all right," Andi said, laughing. "Let's go check out the aquarium store. Maybe we can ask about the missing flame angels, too, while we're there!"

Mr. Martin led the way to Fin Fun, a brightly painted store on a street that ran just behind the waterfront at Coral Point. Andi peered at their display window, which had a selection of energetic little reef fish gliding around in an enormous tank, reminding Andi of Larry Hook's collection. Inside, the store was cool and quiet, with mellow music playing through speakers. The light was soft and watery as the reflections from the fish tanks played across the walls and ceiling of the store.

"May I help you?" a girl with short black hair and a pierced nose asked them. She wore a pale yellow T-shirt with the words FIN FUN printed across the front.

"Sea horses," said Jess promptly. "Do you have any?"

The assistant smiled. "Sure. Our stock is kept in the back." She led them through the store to a large, warehouse-like room at the rear.

As the assistant guided Jess and her dad across to a small tank of sea horses, Andi and Zack took a look around at the other tanks. The fish here were generally smaller than the ones at Mr. Hook's house, but she recognized a number of breeds: wrasses, triggerfish, gobies . . .

"Flame angels!" Andi whispered. She gripped Zack's sleeve and pointed to a small tank in the corner of the room, half hidden by the two enormous tanks on either side. "Look, Zack. Two flame angels!"

Fish not for sale!

Chapter Eight

The two distinctive fish swam slowly around their tank, their neon-bright colors glowing as if they had little light-bulbs inside them. The tank had been tucked into the back of the room as if someone didn't want them to be noticed. Andi hurried over to the tank to get a better look.

"They're a lot like the ones at the SeaLife Center," she said excitedly. "Don't you think?"

"I don't know, Andi," Zack replied. "I mean, unless you're an expert, it's pretty impossible to identify specific fish."

"But two flame angels disappeared from the SeaLife Center," Andi whispered. "And now here are two flame angels tucked out of sight at the back of an aquarium store. Don't you think that's a bit of a coincidence?"

"I'm afraid those fish aren't for sale." The spiky-haired assistant who had been helping Jess and her dad was standing several feet away from them, opening a shiny new water thermometer and slipping it into a tank full of luminous yellow fish. "But if you like angels, I have some angelfish you can take a look at."

"Where did you get these fish?" Andi demanded.

The assistant busied herself with the thermometer. "Don't ask me," she said. "You want Ozzie, the store owner."

"Okay," Andi said. "Can you get him for us, please?"

"He's out right now on a delivery, but he'll be back later," the assistant replied. She carefully fixed the thermometer to the side of the tank.

Jess bounced over to Andi and Zack with Mr. Martin close behind her. "Dad's going to buy some sea horses!" she told them triumphantly.

"That's not quite what I said," Mr. Martin corrected. "I said, I'm going to talk to your mom and we'll take it from there. And we would have to get the tank set up, Jess. It can take weeks or months to get a marine tank ready with the right balance of salts and a steady temperature."

"I don't mind waiting," Jess promised. "Please, could you talk to Mom and see what she says?"

"Okay, I'll talk to her this afternoon," Mr. Martin said. "Now, is everyone ready to go?"

"Look, Jess!" Andi whispered, showing her friend the two flame angels swimming in the tank behind them. "And the assistant says they aren't for sale!"

Jess's eyes widened. "Are they the missing ones?" she asked.

"I don't know," Andi admitted. "It's a strange coincidence, but I don't know how we can prove they're the ones from the SeaLife Center." She paused to stare at the two glowing flame angels darting back and forth. "Zack is right. It's almost impossible to tell the difference between fish of the same breed."

Jess nodded as she gazed into the tank. "Yeah. These guys look exactly the same to me. How are we ever going to know if they're the stolen ones?"

Andi shrugged, still staring at the swimming fish. Just like in Laser's case . . . she had no clue what to do next.

On Thursday morning, Mrs. Talbot called early to say that she and her friend Margot were back from Key West.

"I've got so much to tell you, Mom!" said Andi.

"Save it for ten o'clock!" Mrs. Talbot said mysteriously. "I'll meet you and Jess at the boat-tour ticket office in the marina. Be sure to come wearing your bathing suit, and prepare for a surprise!"

Excited about seeing her mom and finding out about the surprise, Andi finished her breakfast at super speed. Buddy, who was exhausted from playing with Jess's little brothers for most of the previous afternoon, hardly raised his head from his bed when Andi put her plate and mug in the dishwasher and ran upstairs to get ready.

"So what exactly did your mom say about this surprise?" Jess asked as she put on her new swimsuit and threw a pretty little shift dress over the top.

"Not much." Andi pulled on her bathing suit, then wriggled into a T-shirt and shorts. "Just to come wearing the right stuff and not be late. Maybe it's a ride on one of those inflatable bananas we keep seeing out in the bay!"

"Or a boat trip out to see dolphins!" Jess's eyes were as bright with anticipation as Andi's. She pulled on her beach shoes and shouldered her bag. "We've got to go. It's nine-thirty already!"

Mrs. Talbot was waiting for them as arranged, looking tanned and relaxed as she stood beside the boat-trip ticket office. She was with a young dark-skinned woman in a yellow bikini. Andi didn't recognize the woman.

Mrs. Talbot swept Andi into a warm hug, then turned to the woman. "This is Anita Cruz," she said. "She's going to be your instructor for the morning."

"Instructing us in *what*?" asked Andi, baffled.

Anita's face creased with amusement. "I'm a snorkeling teacher," she explained. "Your mom arranged a lesson for the two of you."

"Snorkeling!" Andi had been snorkeling before, when she'd lived in Coral Point, but never out on a coral reef. Her mom had always said she was too young to be away from the beach before. "I can't wait!" she cried.

As they walked down the marina with Anita, Andi told her mom all about Laser, the missing German shepherd, and the disappearing flame angels at the SeaLife Center.

"Leave it to you to find trouble . . . or *animals,* I should say." Judy Talbot smiled. "Well, you'll be glad to hear that Margot and I did nothing except lie on a perfect Key West beach for two days. No excitement for us at all! And no music, either," she added in a low voice to Andi, making her laugh.

Anita took them for a quick snorkeling lesson in an instruction pool tucked behind the marina. She handed them masks and snorkel mouthpieces. Andi pulled down her mask over her eyes and nose and fitted the J-shaped mouthpiece in her mouth. She floated facedown in the pool for a couple of minutes, practicing breathing.

It seemed like a long time since she'd last used a snorkel, and she found the hardest thing was remembering not to panic when the mask leaked water, or when a little water slopped down inside the snorkel and made her splutter. But, knowing that she'd be a long way off the beach at the reef, she took her time and listened carefully to everything Anita was saying. Before they knew it, it was time to go snorkeling for real!

"Remember everything I told you," Anita said, helping Jess and Andi into their safety vests and then lowering them into the warm, shallow water as Mrs. Talbot watched from the side of the boat. "A relaxed snorkeler will always see more, because the marine life will sense that you are not a threat."

Jess put her head down and swam enthusiastically away from the boat—until she crashed into a nearby rock. "Ow!"

"And it's always a good idea to put one hand out in front of you to act as a bumper," Anita added with a grin. "So, any questions?"

"Nope," Andi said. She stuck her masked face into the water and spotted three fish—the front half of their bodies blue and the back half and tails yellow. She lifted her head out of the water and took out her mouthpiece. "Whoa! Did you see those guys?"

Anita took out her own mouthpiece. "Yup. That was Moe, Larry, and Curly—my three favorite bicolor damselfish."

"What do you mean *favorite*?" Jess said, adjusting her mask. "You sound like you know them or something."

"Kind of," Anita admitted. "I see them around here all the time. They stay in a little cove along the reef."

"Can we go look?" Andi asked, really wanting to see the fishes' home.

"Sorry. Damselfish are extremely territorial," Anita told her. "They don't like it when strangers get too close. Especially Moe—he's a fighter."

"Wait a sec." Jess stopped swimming to tread water. "You mean, you can tell the difference between fish of the same breed?" she asked slowly, shooting Andi a look.

"Of course," Anita remarked.

Andi knew just what her friend was thinking. If Anita could tell the difference between damselfish, maybe she could help them figure out if the flame angels at Fin Fun were the missing ones from the SeaLife Center. Andi turned to face Anita. "Can you teach us how to do it, too?"

"Sure." Anita nodded. "Did you have any particular fish in mind?"

"Flame angels," Andi said hopefully.

"I've dived among flames in Hawaii," Anita told her. "We won't see any on this reef, though."

"That doesn't matter," Andi said. "So, how do you tell them apart?"

Anita considered the question. "Flame angel males are generally bigger, and can be more brightly marked," she said. "Then, of course, there's the shape of the fins and tail—large, or perhaps damaged in some way from a fight or a brush with the coral, or consisting of ten or twelve ridges—that kind of thing. Once you start looking, you'll probably be able to find all kinds of unique elements to each fish. Okay, are you kids ready for your first dive?"

Andi pulled down her mask and fitted her mouthpiece. Then, with a thumbs-up signal to Anita and her mom, she ducked just beneath the surface of the sea.

Immediately, a turquoise world opened up before her. Swimming slowly and holding her arm out as a bumper, the way Anita had advised, Andi stared in wonder at the colors of the reef. Red, yellow, blue, and silver fish dashed around the coral, and anemones and seaweed waved softly in the current. Andi spotted fish that looked familiar from Fin Fun and the SeaLife Center—darting wrasses and clown fish, little shrimps on the sandy seabed, and bright yellow gobies.

Trying to remember what Anita had said about setting apart the fish, Andi stared at a group of fish that at

first glance looked identical. Gradually, she began picking out the differences—a longer fin here, a brighter color there. She noticed nicks and tears in a parrot fish's fins and a flash of discoloration on the gleaming flank of a large striped angelfish. The reef was a wonderland of surprises, better than anything Andi could have imagined. For the full half hour of the dive, she felt like a mermaid, swimming through her own private kingdom.

"That was totally magical," Jess sighed, lying on her back next to Andi on the boat as Anita motored back to the marina.

"Totally," Andi agreed. "Thanks, Mom. It was awesome!"

"I'm glad you girls enjoyed it," Mrs. Talbot said. "So, which of the missing pets gets your attention this afternoon?"

"We should probably go back to Fin Fun this afternoon to check on those two fish, while we can still remember what Anita said about telling the difference," Jess announced. "Right, Andi?"

Andi grinned, proud that Jess was getting the hang of pet finding. "Then we can go to the SeaLife Center. I'm sure Shannon or Chad could give us a much more exact description of the missing flame angels, now that we know what we should watch for. Which leaves us plenty of time to look for clues about Laser at the marina."

"No doubt," Jess agreed. "Oh, and while we're at Fin Fun, maybe I can get some more information about sea horses," she added. "Mom isn't totally convinced it's a good idea."

Andi rolled over on her side and looked pleadingly at her mom as Anita brought the motorboat gently into the marina and docked at the jetty. "Will you come with us to the aquarium store, Mom?" she begged. "And then give us a ride to the SeaLife Center? Please? It won't take long. We might find the fish thief before the end of the day!"

Back at Fin Fun, Jess gathered some more information about the sea horses while Andi dragged her mom to the back of the store to show her the little flame angels. She glanced around the room and spotted the small tank tucked away beside a shelving unit. Perched beside it was a sign reading FISH NOT FOR SALE scrawled in large red letters.

To Andi's astonishment, there were now *three* of the brightly colored fish swimming around in the tank.

"I don't believe it!" Andi was stunned. Her mind immediately jumped to the SeaLife Center as she wondered whether they'd had another theft. "There were only two yesterday!"

Mrs. Talbot peered into the tank. "They're beautiful, Andi, but they all look the same to me. Are you sure you can tell the difference?"

Andi stared hard into the water. "That one's the biggest," she said, pointing to a fish that was lurking beside a lump of coral. "He's bright, too. So maybe he's a male. And look at his tail! There's a tiny notch on the top!" She was amazed she hadn't noticed this before, and wondered if this was the extra fish that had been added to the tank in the past twenty-four hours. "The other two are a little paler and smaller. That one's really timid, look." The smallest flame angel was darting nervously through a patch of waving weeds, as if it wanted to avoid the others.

Her mom nodded. "And am I right in thinking that one's got slightly stronger markings over its eyes?" she asked, studying the third fish with interest.

"Yes!" Andi exclaimed, staring at the third flame angel. "They look like little blue eyebrows, Mom!" She pulled out a notebook and scribbled down the information before she forgot it. Then she reached for her digital camera in her shorts pocket and snapped a photo. "Let's see if we can find the manager," she told her mom. "I want to know where he got these fish!"

Andi and her mom joined Jess in the store's main area to look for the owner. But once again, Andi was out of luck. The store clerk said that the owner was out. "I can't *believe* it!" she raged as they left Fin Fun and headed for Mrs. Talbot's rental car. "I mean, how many deliveries does the guy need to make?"

"If he's the thief, he's hardly going to tell you he is, right?" Jess pointed out. "The main thing is that we now have a decent description of the fish, which we can take to the SeaLife Center. And if we check our descriptions against the missing fish, and they're the same," Jess continued, "then he'll *have* to confess."

"Hey, you're pretty good at this stuff," Andi told her. "For a beginner, I mean."

Feeling more cheerful, she climbed into the backseat of her mom's car, and they all set off for the SeaLife Center. But as Andi checked the picture she had snapped of the fish in the screen of her digital camera, her heart sank. The photo was too blurry to pick out the tiny important details. At least she had written the descriptions of the fish in her notebook.

Jess called Zack to give him the latest news. "Zack says he'll call Shannon and let her know we're coming," she said, flipping her phone shut. "But the biggest news is . . ." She paused dramatically.

"Spill," Andi ordered, sitting up straight.

"The biggest news," Jess repeated, "is that there *was* another theft at the SeaLife Center this morning. Zack tried to reach us while we were snorkeling."

Andi felt like leaping out of her seat. "That's too much of a coincidence," she spluttered. "Two fish missing yesterday, three today?"

"*Way* too much," Jess agreed, bouncing with excitement. "So the next question is, how has the thief been taking the fish?"

Andi's mind flipped through everything they knew about the security at the SeaLife Center. "They have guards, security passes, and a security camera system," she said. "Except that some of the security cameras aren't working. But there's staff on duty in every room."

"So there's no way just *anyone* could have gotten away with it," Jess said.

Andi felt a piece of the puzzle suddenly slip into place. "You're exactly right!" Her mouth dropped open as she realized how close they might be coming to the truth. "Not just anyone. Someone in particular. Someone who knows all about how the security works at the aquarium, which cameras work and which don't . . . Someone," she declared triumphantly, "who *works* there!"

Chapter Nine

"See you in half an hour, Mom!" Andi yelled, sliding out of the car and setting off for the steps of the SeaLife Center at top speed, with Jess hot on her heels. She'd almost reached the door when she heard Jess gasp behind her.

"*Laser*! Is that you?" Jess called out.

Andi swung around, her heart suddenly in her mouth, and stared at the dog tethered beside the door. Then . . .

"That's the dog we saw on Monday," she groaned. "Remember? Paler coat, four black paws? I'll bet he belongs to someone who works here."

Jess's face flushed. "Oh," she mumbled. "I forgot about that."

"Hey, it's an honest mistake," Andi reassured her as

they headed into the center. "That dog really does look a lot like Laser." She stopped, thinking about what she had just said. "Remember Ben, at that refreshment stand, who told us he saw Laser running along the marina with Mr. Harding at ten o'clock on Tuesday?" she said. "Two hours after Jim said he'd lost him?" She turned to her friend. "Do you think maybe he saw this dog instead?"

"Maybe," Jess said. "We can ask Shannon if she knows who owns him. But don't forget—the guy said he saw Laser with Mr. Harding."

"Yeah. Let me take a picture of the dog, anyway," Andi suggested. "We can show it to Ben the next time we're at the beach." She pulled out her digital camera and snapped the handsome dog, this time checking to make sure the photo had turned out well, before stepping inside the aquarium.

Shannon was waiting anxiously for them beside the turnstiles.

"No overalls today?" Andi asked, noting that Shannon was wearing an ordinary SeaLife Center polo shirt.

"I don't need them. You'd be surprised at how you can work in an aquarium and not get your hands wet for days at a time!" Shannon ushered them through the gates, and they walked together down the now familiar corridor toward the reef room. "So, Zack tells me you saw three fish at Fin Fun today," she said over her shoulder. "Is that right?"

Andi nodded. "Unfortunately my picture of them turned out blurry, but I've got excellent descriptions in my notebook, right here," she said, patting her bag.

They passed a large photograph on the wall. It showed three long rows of people, all wearing the same Sea-Life Center logo on their blue polo shirts. Andi spotted Shannon and Chad sitting in the front row, smiling out at the camera.

"Is that everyone who works here?" Andi asked, coming to a stop and staring at the picture.

"More or less." Shannon stopped as well. "There are probably a few part-timers who weren't here when the photo was taken. Not my most photogenic day. Why do you ask?"

Andi paused. It was one thing to figure the fish thief might be a member of the staff, but it was a different thing altogether to tell someone who worked at the SeaLife Center herself. What if Shannon was a friend of the thief? It was a horrible thought.

"Do you think it's possible that a staff member might be taking the fish?" Andi put the question as tactfully as she could.

"We thought of that already," Shannon admitted. "I mean, the profile fits, right? Someone who would know which security cameras weren't working and stuff like that. But we check our staff members very carefully. We're as sure as we can be that the thief doesn't work here."

Andi peered more closely at the picture. There was an older-looking man sitting close to Shannon who kind of looked like . . .

"That's weird," Jess spoke up. "Doesn't that man look like Jim Harding?" She pointed to the same man that Andi was inspecting.

"That's Bradley," said Shannon. "He owns Skiff, that gorgeous German shepherd you may have seen outside this morning." She frowned. "You don't suspect *him* of taking the flame angels, do you? Bradley's one of our most senior staff members!"

"Oh, no. Not at all." Jess hurried to reassure her. "He just looks like someone we know."

Shannon seemed relieved, and they moved on down the corridor.

"That's fantastic!" Jess whispered to Andi as they hurried after Shannon. "Not only does the dog look like Laser, but the owner looks like Mr. Harding! We can cross Ben's sighting off our list! It was horrible to think Mr. Harding was lying about Laser, wasn't it?"

Andi knew from past pet-finding experience that it was dangerous to assume anything until they had proof. "We'll see what Ben says when we show him the picture of Skiff," she said cautiously.

As they moved from the carpeted corridor to the reef room, Andi had a strange feeling that there was something she had to remember. She stopped and frowned, staring around at the walls, hoping that the memory would resurface.

"Are you coming?" Jess asked, popping her head back around the corner.

"Uh, yeah," said Andi, a little reluctantly. She started to follow Jess when the memory hit her. She'd had a collision with someone in this exact spot. An employee who had been frazzled and frantic.

"Jess!" she cried. "I have to go back and check that staff photo again!"

Ignoring startled looks from Jess and Shannon, Andi took off back down the corridor like a racehorse. A tall guy, she remembered: blond, with nice eyes—and wet hands. Andi heard Shannon's voice in her head: "You'd be surprised at how you can work in an aquarium and not get your hands wet . . ."

Skidding to a halt beside the staff photo, she eagerly

scanned the rows of faces. There was no sign of the mysterious tall employee.

Suddenly, Andi heard a sound from just behind her. As she turned, she caught a glimpse of the familiar blond head disappearing through a door marked STAFF ONLY. Andi barreled through the door and stared around. There was no one in sight.

Racing back to the reef room as fast as her legs could carry her, Andi burst in on Chad, Shannon, and Jess like a tornado.

"I think I just saw him!" she panted. "The fish thief. He went through the STAFF ONLY door back in the hall!"

"But—" Jess began.

"No time for questions," Andi insisted. "It's him; I'm sure it is. I bumped into him on Monday. Come on, he's getting away!"

Pulling a walkie-talkie off his belt, Chad spoke rapidly into it for a couple of seconds, then thrust it back onto his holster. "That door leads to all the backstage areas in the SeaLife Center," he said as they broke into a run back down the corridor, toward the STAFF ONLY door.

"Backstage?" Jess echoed, her eyes wide. "Like, where you can get to the tanks?"

"Where you can get to the tanks *without the cameras*

seeing you," Shannon said, sounding grim. "How long ago did you see this guy, Andi?"

"Two minutes max." Andi ran on ahead and pushed through the door. "He didn't notice me," she said, glancing over her shoulder at the others. "I'm sure—*oh!*"

She had collided with someone. Someone tall and blond and wearing the royal blue shirt of a SeaLife Center employee.

"Hey!" said the man. He crinkled his hazel eyes in a friendly manner that Andi instantly recognized. "You again? This is getting to be a habit! What are you doing back here, kid? This area is off-limits to the public."

His grin faded when he noticed Chad and Shannon standing at the door with Jess beside them. And then he whirled around into a sprint, his long legs propelling him impossibly fast down the hallway until he was out of sight.

"After him!" Chad shouted.

Andi put on a fresh burst of speed. She and Jess tore down the corridor, trying to avoid startled employees coming the other way. There seemed to be endless things blocking the path—garbage cans in the hall, trolleys, buckets of fish and tubs of food pellets, brooms and open doors—even the occasional chair. *It's like an obstacle course,* Andi thought, vaulting over a broom and hurrying around to the right.

Up ahead, they all heard a crash, followed by a very strong odor of rotting fish.

"P.U.!" Andi held her nose as she skidded to a halt around the next corner. A large tub of fish had been dumped all over the passage—and the guy who'd knocked it down was sprawled full length on the ground, cursing as he struggled to his feet.

"The sea otters' lunch!" Shannon groaned.

"Stop!" Andi yelled as the thief jumped up and sped on down the corridor. "We just want to talk to you!"

"What a stink!" Jess choked, flapping her hand in front of her face as they climbed over the slippery silver mess on the floor. "We'll be able to smell him for miles!"

They'd moved into some kind of warehouse at the back of the aquarium, all high ceilings and tiled floors, with men in hard hats moving pallets of equipment across the floor on forklift trucks.

"Where is he?" Andi groaned, staring around in dismay.

Jess held up her finger. "Smell *that*?" she asked with excitement. The distinct reek of fish was coming from behind a tower of pallets next to the warehouse exit.

Filled with fresh enthusiasm, Andi dashed toward the pallets and found a damp, very smelly SeaLife Center polo shirt lying on the dusty ground. She gingerly grabbed the shirt sopping with fish guts and held it at arm's length as the others ran up beside her. "It was so nasty he had to take it off," she said, trying not to breathe through her nose.

"Ew!" Jess cried, stepping back. "Sea otters like their fish pretty ripe."

Shannon leaned against a barrel and put her hands on her hips. "We lost him!"

"Look at it this way," Andi sighed, turning the T-shirt over in her hands. "At least he left a clue."

Chapter Ten

Andi held up the polo shirt to inspect their only evidence.

"Can I see that for a minute?" Chad asked with a frown.

Andi handed it over, and Chad studied it carefully. He didn't seem too bothered by the smell. "This isn't a SeaLife Center T-shirt," he said, looking up. "It's the wrong shade of blue. It's *almost* right, but not quite."

"And look," Andi said, noticing something else. "The 'i' is missing on 'SeaLife'!" She stared in amazement at the logo, which read SEALFE CENTER.

"This guy must've had the T-shirt printed specially," Chad guessed, "so he could pass as a staff member and walk through the aquarium unnoticed."

"Pretty careless to have a spelling mistake on your disguise," Jess scoffed.

"Guess you're not likely to notice a missing 'i' on a T-shirt if you're *wearing* it," Andi said with a grin. "And even less likely for others to notice it if it's being worn by someone in a hurry."

Three security guards came through the warehouse exit, approaching Chad and shaking their heads. It looked as though the thief had gotten past them, too.

"So, what do you suggest we do next?" Shannon asked.

"Find the T-shirt store," said Jess promptly. "Do you have a phone book in your office, Shannon?"

"Sure," said Shannon. "Let's go check it out!"

Ten minutes later Shannon, Andi, and Jess were staring in dismay at the phone book, which lay open on Shannon's desk.

"There are hundreds of stores!" Jess groaned. "I had no idea T-shirt printing was so popular!"

"I guess we shouldn't be too surprised," Andi sighed. "Coral Point is a tourist town. A T-shirt is a classic tourist souvenir, isn't it? Print a T-shirt with a photo from your vacation to take home and show all your friends. It's no good, guys. We'll have to think of a different approach."

Jess's cell phone rang. She opened it up and held it to

her ear. "Hi, Zack," she said gloomily. "Do you want the good news or the bad news?"

"There's nothing more you can do here," Shannon told Andi while Jess filled Zack in on the latest news. "Listen, you've only got a couple days of your vacation left, right? If I were you, I'd head down to the beach and have a little fun. You've been amazingly helpful. We'll track down some descriptions of the missing fish and follow up that lead about the fish store that you gave us. You can leave it to us now, okay?"

Andi really didn't want to leave it unsolved. They'd followed this case so faithfully

"Zack's going to meet us at Gianello's," Jess said, slipping her phone back into her pocket. "It's getting pretty late. Maybe we should do what Shannon says and leave the rest to the SeaLife Center. Remember, we've still got to find Laser."

"I guess," Andi said reluctantly, but she knew Jess was right about Laser. She turned to Shannon. "You will tell us if you find out anything else, won't you?"

"Of course we will," Shannon promised.

Andi's phone bleeped. It was a text message.

ARE YOU COMING? I'VE BEEN IN THE PARKING LOT FOR FIFTEEN MINUTES! MOM

Andi spotted another SeaLife Center brochure lying

on Shannon's desk. Andi tucked her phone away and picked it up. "Mind if I take this?" she asked Shannon.

"Go ahead," said Shannon. "I'll give Zack a call later if we have news."

Andi and Jess trooped slowly out of the aquarium and greeted Andi's mom in the parking lot.

"Why the long faces?" Judy Talbot asked, holding open the door to the rental car so that they could climb in the back. "Didn't the descriptions fit?"

"We didn't have time to match descriptions," Andi admitted. "We got a little distracted when the thief showed up."

"What?"

They took turns telling Mrs. Talbot what had happened at the aquarium as they drove back through town and out to the waterfront. It had all been pretty exciting, Andi had to admit. It was just so frustrating that they'd *still* hit a brick wall in the end.

Zack was waiting for them as arranged, pacing beside Gianello's ice-cream stand on the waterfront and clutching a half-eaten strawberry cone.

"I don't believe you chased the guy and didn't catch him!" he groaned as Andi and Jess sat down.

"You don't have to rub it in." Andi glanced at the guy working the stand. "Can I get a chocolate fudge cone over here, please?"

"Make it two," Jess added.

They settled at their familiar table near the water. Automatically, Andi glanced around in case Laser was waiting for a bite of someone's cone. But there was no coppery dog on the boardwalk. Her heart felt like it was somewhere down in the tip of her sneaker. Even the thought of a Gianello's chocolate fudge cone couldn't cheer Andi up right now.

"Shannon will let me know about the flame angels, Andi," said Zack, noticing Andi's expression. "And I'll pass it on as soon as I can."

"But it's not the same as solving the case ourselves," Andi said. "I wish I wasn't going home on the weekend. Then maybe we could see this case through to the end."

"We've still got the Laser case," Jess pointed out. "And if we haven't found him by Sunday morning, I promise we'll keep looking. I'll e-mail you every day with updates."

With a heavy sigh, Andi accepted the chocolate fudge cone that the ice-cream attendant brought over to her.

"Hey, mister," Zack said, pointing to the guy's hat, "your cap—"

"I know, I know," the ice-cream guy muttered. "It's spelled wrong."

As soon as he said it, Andi's ears perked up.

"I didn't realize it until someone else pointed it out to me yesterday. We only got these caps delivered on Tuesday!" The man pulled off the green cap and stared sourly at the logo.

"Can I take a look at that?" Andi reached for the cap and studied it carefully. It read: GANELLO'S. "The 'i' is missing!" she realized. "Just like on the fake SeaLife Center shirt!"

Jess snatched the cap from Andi. "Yeah. It should say Gianello's! Where did you get this thing printed?"

"A place called *Tee for Me*, beside the tourist information center," the man said. "We won't be going back there, that's for sure. Keep the hat if you want. I'm sick of having it pointed out to me all day."

Andi slapped some money down on the table to cover the bill. Then she and Jess jumped up and broke into a run down the boardwalk, toward the tourist information center.

"Wait! Come back!" Zack shouted, following Andi and Jess as they wove neatly through the crowds on the boardwalk. "I want to finish my ice cream!"

"Sorry, Zack!" Andi shouted, swerving to avoid a startled-looking old lady in a floppy purple sun hat. "Looks like you'll have to eat and run!"

* * *

Tee for Me was a boxy-looking store beside the tourist information center. Its plain doorway was shaded by a large palm tree. There were a couple of faded T-shirts printed with Florida sunsets in the window and a long line of people at the desk inside. "Look at all these people," Jess moaned, making a face.

"I guess we'll just have to wait our turn," Andi said, disappointed. Then she brightened up. "But at least it'll give us time to eat our ice cream."

While they waited, they watched the harassed-looking man behind the counter. He was short and skinny with a mop of sandy hair, and he was scurrying behind the counter, fetching order forms and color samples and occasionally disappearing into the back of the store to answer the phone. Whenever he reappeared, he cast a horrified look at the line of customers, which was growing longer by the minute.

"Poor guy," Zack said. "He looks rushed off his feet."

"We'd like to order a blue T-shirt," Andi said when they reached the front of the line about half an hour later. "Could you print 'SeaLife Center' on it for us?"

"How long will we have to wait?" Jess asked.

The guy shrugged. "Can't say for sure. I'm really busy. There are supposed to be four of us working here but

Tony called in sick this morning, Cara quit last week for a job where she gets to sit down once in a while, and Marion got fired for bad spelling. To be honest, you'd get this quicker if you went for airbrushing or silk-screening. Wouldn't you rather have a photo printed on the shirt? You wouldn't have to wait for me to do it." He glanced over his shoulder, and Andi saw two people at work in the room behind the store. "Mike and Izzy do all the pictures. Me, I do all the lettering!"

"Sorry," Andi said. "It's lettering we want."

The guy sighed, then pushed across a piece of paper for them to fill in. Andi took great care to spell *SeaLife Center* correctly.

"I don't get it," Zack said, peering over Andi's shoulder. "You could just buy a SeaLife Center shirt in the aquarium gift shop."

Over the clunking and whirring of the embroidery machine behind the counter, Andi explained what the printing error meant. "If we can prove the SeaLife Center T-shirt came from here, then maybe we can get a location for the thief!" she said. She handed the completed form to the attendant. "If you could possibly do it quickly, we'd be really grateful," she said.

He nodded. "Come back in twenty minutes or so. I'll try to get it done for you by then."

"That'd be fantastic!" Andi whooped. "Thanks very much."

Exactly twenty minutes later, they headed back to the T-shirt store. The line was as long as ever, but to Andi's relief, the guy who'd taken their order spotted them and motioned them forward. "That's twelve fifty." He pushed the T-shirt across the counter and held out his hand for payment.

"Thanks." Andi paid the guy. She took the T-shirt and unfolded it very carefully. There, printed right across the middle, were the words SEALFE CENTER.

"It's spelled wrong," she said with a happy grin.

"You're kidding. Darn machine!" the attendant grumbled, taking the T-shirt from her and holding it up to the light. "We got a repair guy in to fix the broken 'i' key on the embroidery computer just yesterday. I guess he didn't fix it at all." He smiled apologetically. "I'm so busy I don't get time to check every shirt. If the customer doesn't notice, I'm afraid mistakes can get overlooked."

"That's okay," Andi said. "Believe it or not, we wanted it to be broken."

The attendant looked at her as if she were nuts. "Huh?"

"Listen," said Jess, leaning across the desk. "Have you done another SeaLife Center shirt lately?"

The attendant frowned. "Sure," he said. "A guy came in—when was it now? Just last weekend, I guess."

"Could you describe him?" Andi asked eagerly.

The attendant puffed out his cheeks. "Are you kidding me? I get about two hundred people in here a day."

"He might have been tall and blond," Andi suggested. "And he might have been hanging about in a kind of fishy way."

The attendant laughed. "Fishy! Yeah, I do remember him. Wearing a shirt with FIN FUN splashed across the front. If you hadn't said 'fishy,' I'd never have remembered. About six feet tall, blondish hair, and around my age, maybe?"

Sounded like their thief! Andi felt like leaping over the counter and hugging him.

"I don't suppose he left a delivery address?" Zack asked.

"Picked it up himself right then and there, so no delivery address," the attendant said. He glanced past them at the growing line. "Look, I have to get back to work."

"Here's fifteen dollars for the T-shirt. Keep the change!" Andi said. "You've been a huge help!"

"I don't have to ask where we're headed next," said Zack, following Andi and Jess as they sprinted out of the T-shirt printing store. "Fin Fun, right?"

"What are we going to do if the guy's there?" Jess asked on the way down the boardwalk. "He'll recognize us, Andi!"

"He won't know Zack," Andi said, thinking fast as they headed down an alley into the little street of stores that ran behind the waterfront. "He'll have to cover for us."

The kids skidded to a halt a couple of doors down from Fin Fun. Andi's heart was racing, and she tried to breathe normally. If the thief was in the store, they couldn't draw attention to themselves, and they might need to be ready to chase him again. "Okay, here's the plan," she said after a moment. "Zack, you go in and scout out the store. If you see a tall guy with blond hair and hazel eyes, come out and tell us. We'll call Shannon and tell her to get the police over here."

"There might still be some mistake," Zack pointed out. "We haven't figured out for sure if these are the same fish. Plus, a lot of people are six feet tall and blond."

"Well, we have more coincidences: three flame angels disappearing from the SeaLife Center and three flame angels mysteriously appearing at Fin Fun, the fake SeaLife Center shirt being ordered by a guy wearing a Fin Fun shirt . . ." She stopped to think about it. "Wait! There's one more thing that would give us our proof once and for all."

"What is it?" Jess prompted.

"This!" Andi pulled out the SeaLife Center brochure she'd taken from Shannon's desk. She studied the photograph on the front, the picture of the flame angels that had first caught her attention on Monday. Scanning the picture slowly, she picked out a fish that was more brightly colored than the others. Even from a photograph, the little notch on his tail was clearly visible—the same notch that she had seen on the flame angel at the back of the store. "It's a match," Andi said, pointing to the picture. "I'm sure of it." She tucked the brochure back into her bag.

"Cool!" Jess pushed Zack through the door. "Go on. You might overhear something useful!"

Zack entered the store, looking a little nervous, and Andi and Jess loitered on the sidewalk. Andi peered through the store window, hanging back as best she could. Her heart jumped into her mouth when she spotted a tall, blond man talking urgently to the spiky-haired assistant.

Zack came hurrying out. "He's in there," he said. "Quick, make the call!"

Jess pulled out her cell phone and began dialing the number Zack gave her.

Andi made a split-second decision. "I'm going in," she said, and started making her way up the steps.

"But you can't!" Jess spluttered. "He'll recognize you for sure!"

"I'll keep my head down," Andi said, sounding braver than she felt. "I have to hear what they're talking about!"

Pulling the misspelled Gianello's cap from her bag, she put it on and tugged it down low. Then she quietly and gently slipped in the door, pulling it shut behind her. She tiptoed to a quiet corner of the store where she could hang around unnoticed but still hear the discussion.

"You *sold* one?" the blond thief was hissing at the spiky-haired girl. "How could you do that? I *told* you not to sell them!"

"The guy offered me a hundred bucks," said the girl, twisting her nose stud nervously. "He went on and on at me, TJ. . . . He wouldn't take no for an answer! Listen, you've still got two more in the tank."

"These aren't goldfish, Karen," the thief spat out. "These are beautiful, wild-caught Hawaiian flame angels, stolen to order, for *three* hundred bucks apiece. Mr. Hook chose them himself from the aquarium, and he's a guy who knows his fish. What am I supposed to say to him? He already freaked when I told him I couldn't get the fourth one."

Andi had trouble suppressing a gasp. *Larry Hook had ordered the thefts?*

"I'm sorry, TJ," the girl said, twisting her nose stud again. "Look, I got a little nervous. Even though you said the best place to hide fish was in a bunch of *other* fish, people started noticing the flames and asking about them. I'm supposed to be taking care of the store for Ozzie this week. He'd kill me if he knew I was hiding stolen fish here."

"Where *else* were we supposed to keep them? All the equipment to take care of them is right here." He began to pace in front of her. "Man, that money was almost in my hands!"

Andi glanced toward the door. Jess was pointing at her watch and holding up five fingers. Backup would arrive in five minutes. Andi prayed that the thief would keep talking just a little longer.

The blond guy pushed past Karen and headed out to the back room. The girl followed him, apologizing again and again. After a short pause, Andi followed, keeping the brim of her cap pulled down. She peeked through the doorway.

The thief stopped beside the flame angels' tank, which Andi noticed was still tucked beside the shelving unit. He shook his head in disgust. "Man, you sold the big one, too," he said. "I was hoping to press an extra fifty out of Hook for that beauty."

Andi tiptoed into the room and slunk behind a shelving unit and out of sight. She edged close to the tank of stolen fish. Carefully peeking into the tank, she could make out the two paler flame angels still swimming around. She pulled out the SeaLife brochure and studied it carefully. A pair of paler flames were tucked down at the bottom of the picture: a timid-looking one and another with dark blue "eyebrows."

Looks like Karen sold the one with the notch in its tail, Andi decided. But she was confident that she could identify the other two stolen fish from the photo. She tucked the brochure back into her bag and checked her watch. Surely five minutes must have passed by now?

Suddenly, the thief gave a roar of rage. "Who's that?"

Andi broke cover, sprinting through the stockroom, losing her Gianello's cap as she ran.

"It's the kid from the aquarium!" the thief yelled.

Andi dodged through the tanks, her heart thundering like a steam engine. The thief was taller and clumsier, and she could hear him knocking into the tanks as he ran after her. The girl was shouting something, but the storefront was getting nearer. . . .

Then Andi felt the thief's hand land on her shoulder! In a desperate gesture of self-defense, she flung her bag behind her. She heard a satisfying *clunk* and a yell as the thief tripped over the bag and went sprawling . . . right at the feet of two large police officers standing by the store counter.

"Andi!" Jess seized Andi's arm as she stumbled out of the way. "Are you okay?"

Andi took in the wonderful sight of Jess's concerned face and Shannon and Chad both standing at the door of Fin Fun. Behind them, Zack was looking on anxiously, lit up by the flashing lights of a squad car parked in the road. The officers had already pinned the thief to the floor, and Karen, the shop assistant, was being cuffed as they watched.

"I'm fine," Andi said, her legs still trembling. "But boy, do I have some stuff to tell you. . . ."

Chapter Eleven

Shannon and Chad had brought a portable battery-operated heater with them so the flame angels could be transported safely back to the aquarium. They carried the tank carefully to their van making sure they wouldn't spill any water. Once there, they stuck the heater inside the tank and switched it on.

"Won't the water come over the top while you're driving?" Zack asked.

"Not with this," Shannon said. She pulled out a sheet of stiff polyethylene.

Chad measured the fish tank opening and they marked the dimensions on the polyethylene, then cut along the lines with a craft knife. "Perfect," Shannon said, laying the custom cover over the tank and taping it in place. "It's not exactly rocket science, but it'll keep the fish safe."

"Shouldn't the water be exposed to the air so the fish get the oxygen they need?" Andi asked.

"We couldn't take them on a long journey like this," Chad explained, "but we'll be back at the SeaLife Center in about five minutes. They'll be absolutely fine." He watched the flame angels swimming to and fro and then smiled at Andi, Jess, and Zack. "You kids have been fantastic," he said. "Thank you so much."

"It was an impressive piece of detective work," Shannon said. "I wouldn't want to be a criminal with you three around."

"I'm just glad the fish will be back with the others," Andi said.

Shannon and Chad climbed into the front of the van. "Thanks for everything!" they called as Shannon drove carefully away.

"Wow! What an ending!" Zack said.

"Being a pet detective is the best!" Jess exclaimed. "Now let's see what's happening inside the store."

The rest of the afternoon and much of the early evening passed in a blur of police, questions, and official activity. Though Jess and Zack were eventually sent home, Andi and her mom stayed behind. The police were extremely interested in hearing about Larry Hook's part in the thefts, and at the police station, Andi reported the conversation she'd overheard word for word. Basically, Larry Hook had asked TJ to steal the exact fish he'd wanted from the SeaLife Center. Andi guessed Anita wasn't the only local person who could tell fish apart!

At last, Andi and her mom stepped out of the station, just as the sun was setting over the marina and casting a warm orange glow across the sea.

"It's too late to look for Laser now, I guess," Andi said as they headed to the car. "We'll all have to go down to the marina first thing tomorrow morning."

"Oh, Andi . . ." Mrs. Talbot shook her head in despair. "You just solved one crime. Don't you think you need a break?"

"Laser's still missing, Mom!" Andi pointed out, chewing her thumbnail. "It's pretty hard to take a break knowing that."

"Well, I'll be staying at the Martins' tonight and tomorrow, so at least I can be with you," said Mrs. Talbot, starting up the car. "But I'm going to *insist* that you relax for the rest of the evening, Andi. We're having a barbecue tonight. This is still our vacation, after all. If you want to look for Laser tomorrow, then I'll just have to live with it. Deal?"

Andi managed a sheepish smile. "Okay," she said. "Deal."

* * *

On Friday morning, Andi woke up early to the feeling of Buddy's cold nose sniffing at her neck. Feeling relaxed and refreshed after a great evening of food and poolside games, she stroked the little terrier's rough head and lay back for a moment, thinking about the drama of the day before. *One case solved; one more to go,* she thought, determined to find Laser without any further delay.

Zack was already waiting for them when Andi, Jess, and Buddy turned up on his doorstep an hour later.

"Hopefully we'll catch some different boat owners in the marina today," Andi said. "Do you have that picture of Skiff that we took yesterday at the aquarium, Jess?"

"I printed a copy on Dad's computer," Jess said, handing it over.

"And I have the sandwich boards," Zack said. "Let's go!"

They walked the familiar route to the beach, talking over the events of the day before as they went.

"I can't believe we went to Larry Hook's house and didn't even suspect him," Jess said, shaking her head. "Hey, maybe the rest of his fish collection was stolen to order, too!"

Jess shrugged. "Still, I feel a little bad for him, since he's the one who taught me about sea horses. Dad's ordered a pair. The tank's being delivered on Monday and we can collect the sea horses as soon as it's all set up!"

Andi felt a stab of sadness that she wouldn't be in Coral Point on Monday to help Jess prepare for her new pets. Keeping up their friendship long-distance was worth it, that was for sure, but like her mom said, there had to be compromises.

Andi thought she was seeing things when a lively young German shepherd suddenly bounced into the road in front of them. Buddy barked with delight and frisked around the shepherd's long legs as the bigger dog sniffed at him in a friendly manner.

"Rosie!" A woman came running out into the street, looking anxious. "Come back here! I'm so sorry," she said, restraining the lively young dog with some difficulty. "Rosie is crazy about kids, and mine are staying with friends for Spring Break. I guess their dog misses them. Hey, steady now!"

Rosie bounced a little more, panting happily at Andi and the others, who laughed and petted her for a moment or two.

"She was gorgeous," Jess sighed as the woman dragged the enthusiastic German shepherd away from them at last. "I thought it was Laser for a minute."

"Me, too," Zack agreed. "I never knew there were so many German shepherds in Coral Point!"

Tugging on Buddy's leash to bring the little terrier to heel, Andi was thoughtful as they headed on toward the beach. It was true that there seemed to be a lot of German shepherds around—enough to muddy the waters in their search for Laser. Perhaps Bradley and his dog Skiff *weren't* the solution to the refreshment guy's sighting at the marina after all. Perhaps it was all more complicated than that.

Andi was still puzzling over the problem when they reached the stand.

"Any luck on Laser yet?" asked Ben sympathetically, tipping back his red cap as he spoke. "I've been looking for him ever since I saw you the other day, but I haven't seen a thing."

Jess held out the photograph of Skiff. "Is this the dog you saw on Tuesday morning?" she asked, passing it over.

The guy shook his head. "That's not Laser," he said. "I definitely saw Laser."

Jess's face fell. "But—"

Andi jumped in quickly. "What makes you so sure that you saw *Laser* that morning?" she prompted.

"I told you," said Ben. "He was running after Jim

Harding. He's a distinctive dog with his copper foot and that gorgeous coat. And before you ask, I don't need glasses!"

Andi suddenly thought of a different way of asking the question. "What makes you so sure that you saw *Jim Harding* that morning?" she said slowly, allowing the cogs to whir in her mind.

"Jim?" Ben echoed. He looked surprised. "Well, I guess I thought it was Jim because . . . well, he was with Laser. Anyone would think that, wouldn't they?"

Andi pounced. "So, you're not sure?"

"He was wearing his usual Coral Point Marina T-shirt and running shorts," Ben said defensively. "Sure, it was him." But he didn't sound sure at all.

The kids thanked him for his help and headed down the boardwalk.

"I think we've been looking at this the wrong way," Andi declared as they sat swinging their legs over the boardwalk. Buddy chased his tail briefly on the sand, then flopped down in the shade by Andi's feet. "I think Ben really *did* see Laser at ten o'clock on Tuesday morning—but Laser was following *someone else*."

"What about the description of Jim's clothes?" Zack chimed in.

Andi turned to him. "A Coral Point Marina T-shirt and

shorts! How many people must wear that combination around here? It's not exactly original."

As if to prove Andi's point, a woman ran past in a pink version of the marina T-shirt, her running shorts gleaming white against her tanned legs.

Jess jumped to her feet, throwing down her bag in frustration. "This is ridiculous!" she said. "We're not getting anywhere!" Her bag flew open on the boardwalk, scattering photos on the sandy planks.

Zack leaned over and picked up the photographs. "Hey, are those the pictures we took on Sunday?" he asked with interest.

"Yeah," said Jess grumpily. "I forgot to tell you that I printed them out, too, while you were still at the police station, Andi."

Andi leaned over and studied the pictures in Zack's hands. There were some really funny ones, which brought a smile to her face: she and Jess posing on the beach and jumping over the waves and pouting beside the *Lemming* . . .

Andi snatched a photograph of the *Lemming* and stared at it. She and Jess were striking crazy film-star poses in the foreground, while in the background Carl and Sara Lem were standing against the cruiser's railing and smiling down on the action. Carl was wearing dark

sunglasses, a royal blue Coral Point Marina T-shirt, and white shorts.

"I want to ask Ben another question," Andi said, scrambling to her feet and taking care not to let go of the precious photo. "I think I'm on to something, you guys. Come on!"

They ran back down the boardwalk to the refreshment stand.

"You again!" Ben leaned on the counter and sighed in a good-natured, joking way. "How many more questions?"

Andi thrust the photograph of Carl Lem under his nose. "Could you have seen *this* man with Laser on Tuesday morning instead?" she demanded. "Notice the Coral Point Marina T-shirt and shorts?"

Ben frowned. "I don't know." He squinted at the picture. "The clothes are right . . . so is the build. I only saw him from the back, so maybe—yes. This is Carl Lem, isn't it? He owns the *Lemming*."

"See?" Andi swung around triumphantly to Jess and Zack, who were both looking confused. "*Laser* could have mistaken Carl for Jim, and followed *him* into the marina!"

"Surely Laser would know what Jim looks like?" Jess objected.

"Maybe not," Andi insisted. "Not from a distance. Don't forget, Jim doesn't own Laser. He's just been taking care of him while his daughter is away!"

"Wow, Andi." Zack's eyes brightened. "You could be right."

Andi hoped so. She scouted the marina for the *Lemming*. They had to ask the Lems about Laser!

"But if you're looking for the *Lemming*, you're out of luck." Ben interrupted her thoughts. "They left yesterday on a cruise around the islands. They'd been stocking the boat for days, so I think it was going to be a long trip."

Andi groaned. "Three weeks!" she said, remembering the conversation they'd had with the Lems just the morning before. "It's part of their honeymoon!" Then she remembered something else. "Remember how Buddy ran onto the *Lemming*, and we thought he'd smelled the Lems' stock of food?" she gasped. "What if he smelled *Laser* instead?"

Zack frowned. "Are you saying that the Lems stole Laser?"

"I'm sure they didn't take him on purpose," Andi said, shaking her head. "But what if Laser followed Carl, and then somehow got trapped aboard their boat?"

Jess sat down rather suddenly. "Great," she said. "If

Laser's out at sea, how are we supposed to find him?"

"Hey!" Zack tapped Andi on the arm. "Isn't that Jim Harding coming this way?"

Andi whirled around. Running toward them were two men—and one of them was the familiar figure of the yachting-supply shop owner.

"Mr. Harding!" Andi waved frantically to attract his attention. "Over here!"

Jim Harding saw them. He and his companion immediately slowed down. "Any news today?" he asked as he tried to catch his breath.

"We think we've figured it out," Andi said, trying to control her excitement. She outlined their theory about the Lems in seconds flat. And then had to repeat it.

Jim Harding listened, the fresh light of hope in his eyes. "That's some theory," he said when Andi had finished the second time. He turned to his companion. "What do you think, Ed?"

The second man nodded. "Sounds possible to me." He extended his hand and introduced himself. "Ed Harding, Jim's brother. I've heard a lot about you kids."

"But what can we do?" Jess said after all the introductions had been made. "Laser's at sea and we're on shore!"

"We go to the harbormaster's office and radio the

Lemming," Mr. Harding said, breaking into a run once more. "Follow me!"

The harbormaster's office was in a neat white clapboard building beside the main jetty. It was clear that the harbormaster knew the Hardings, and Andi held her breath as he swiftly radioed the call.

"Mr. Lem, this is Steve Mackinnon, harbormaster at Coral Point. This may sound like a strange question, but do you have a dog named Laser on board?"

Carl Lem's familiar voice crackled through a speaker. "Yes!" he said, sounding astonished. "We just discovered him belowdecks about an hour ago and were about to call in ourselves! How the heck did you know?"

"Call it a lucky guess." The harbormaster smiled. "You probably won't believe the story, anyway." He leaned over the desk and shook hands with an ecstatic Jim Harding, and the whole office erupted with delight.

"You were right, Andi!" Jess squealed, whirling Andi into a dance.

"Fantastic detective work, Andi," Zack said, his face creased into one huge smile.

"Hold up, guys. I can't take all the credit!" Andi laughed as Buddy caught the air of excitement in the room and started chasing his tail in circles. "We worked as a team all the way."

"What can I say?" Mr. Harding shook Andi's hand enthusiastically, then shook hands with the others as well. "You've just mended my daughter's heart—and saved my dog-sitting reputation. Well done, all three of you!"

The harbormaster, who was still talking to Carl Lem on the radio, turned around with his hand over the receiver. "Mr. Lem offered to wait for you at Pelican Island so he can return the dog," he said. "Can you take the *Happy Jack* out there this afternoon, Jim?"

"In a heartbeat," Mr. Harding said with a broad smile. He turned to Andi and the others. "I guess now would be a good time to offer you that trip out to sea. You can call your folks and ask them along. What do you think?"

Andi, Jess, and Zack all scrambled for their phones.

"We found Laser!" Andi babbled into the receiver as soon as her mom answered. "Well, we know where he is—a place called Pelican Island—and Mr. Harding's offered to take us there in his boat. And you're invited, too, Mom!"

"A sailing trip?" Mrs. Talbot sounded delighted. "Sounds perfect, Andi. Maybe we'll get to spend some time together on our vacation after all!"

Chapter Twelve

Andi closed her eyes and stood at the stern of the *Happy Jack*, feeling the warm southerly wind blowing through her hair. Tied up snugly in a special canine life jacket, Buddy lay at her feet. They'd been sailing toward Pelican Island for more than two hours, and the waters were limpid and blue. Darting fish chased one another beneath the bows, and Andi craned her neck, hoping to see some dolphins, while the sails billowed behind her and the salty smell of the sea rose up all around.

"This is the life." Judy Talbot climbed up the cabin steps and passed Andi a cold drink. "How much farther to Pelican Island, do you think?"

"I was just studying the chart with Mr. Harding," Andi said, before taking a long gulp of lemonade. "He says we should be there in about twenty minutes."

"How's Zack?" Mrs. Talbot asked sympathetically. "He looked pretty green for a while there."

Andi glanced at Zack, who was lying very still in a shady spot at the side of the boat. "I think he'd rather be playing tennis right now," she said with a grin.

Jess and her mom ducked beneath the sail and bounced over to Andi.

"Isn't this the best?" Jess said, her eyes shining. "I could sail all day long."

"Okay!" Mr. Harding called, ducking expertly as the boom swung over his head. "Face forward, guys! Can you see that strip of land ahead? Pelican Island, here we come!"

The narrow strip of land grew larger as Andi watched, the tiny palm trees and wash of breaking waves along the shoreline gradually becoming visible. There was a small marina, where five or six different boats were moored. With a fresh rush of excitement, Andi picked out the distinctive, sleek shape of the *Lemming*. Carl Lem waved at them from the railing of the cruiser, grinning broadly as Andi and the others waved back. And beside him, leaping with delight along the deck, was Laser.

There was a sloop-sized space just on the far side of the *Lemming*. Jim Harding and his brother expertly steered the *Happy Jack* into position, in a whirl of ropes

and sails and the grinding sound of the anchor dropping to the soft, sandy seabed. With a gentle bump, the *Happy Jack* came alongside. Mr. Harding vaulted off the sloop and onto the *Lemming,* where Laser gave him the kind of welcome that would have knocked over a smaller man.

It wasn't long before Andi, Jess, and Zack had joined them aboard the *Lemming.* Mrs. Talbot and Buddy brought up the rear, the little terrier wriggling impatiently at the sight of the big German shepherd.

"It's great to see you, Laser!" Andi dropped to her knees and flung her arms around the tail-wagging dog. "You scared us, vanishing like that!"

"He'd gotten himself locked in the galley," Sara Lem explained, petting and stroking Laser's ears as Laser whined and wriggled with delight at all the attention. "We had dinner with friends on a nearby island last night, so we only discovered him this morning when we headed belowdeck for breakfast."

". . . And found Laser lying in a mess of bread crumbs and cereal!" Carl Lem added with a grin. "If a dog's going to get stuck anywhere on a boat, I guess the galley is a good place!"

"I'm so sorry for all the trouble," Mr. Harding said.

"Please, let me pay for any food Laser ate, and any damage he caused to your boat."

Carl Lem waved his hand. "Don't worry about that," he said. "We have more than enough of everything aboard and there was no damage. I'm just glad that you have Laser back, safe and sound."

Laser gave a deep throaty bark and raced joyously around the deck with Buddy in hot pursuit.

"Pet finding is totally cool," Jess said as they stood and watched the dogs play in the Pelican Island sunshine. "You know what, Andi? Zack and I have been talking, and we thought we could set up a Florida pet-finding club of our own, now that we've learned so much from an expert!"

Andi stared at Jess. "Really?" she said, delighted. "You'll do that?"

"Sure we will!" Zack said. "And we'll keep you up to date with everything we do so you can give us pointers."

"What will Chloe and Suki think?" Andi asked, only half joking.

"Who cares?" Jess said airily. "They wouldn't know a good time if it came up and bit them on their perfectly tanned noses."

Over Jess's shoulder, Andi could see the turquoise ocean spreading to the horizon, glinting and swelling with its own special beauty. Something broke the surface of the water, and Andi stared in delight as three dolphins leaped into view, curling themselves over and down again into the waves in perfect unison.

She turned to Jess and gave her a fierce hug. "Friends forever?" she said.

Jess hugged her back. "Forever and ever!"